FALLEN CREST CAMPOUT

A FALLEN CREST / CREW CROSSOVER NOVELLA

TIJAN

Edited by: Jessica Royer Ocken
Edited by: Paige Smith
Proofread by: Amy English and Chris O'Neil Parece
Beta read by: Crystal R Solis and Rochelle Paige

NOTE TO THE READER

I'd previously written a Mason Kade bonus scene.
The timeline for that scene takes place much later after this
novella.

Timeline for this novella is after:
Fallen Crest Forever
Crew
The Boy I Grew Up With
(set during the summer right before the end of Crew Princess)

1

SAMANTHA

"I don't like this."

A hand went to the back of my chair, a head popped up between our two front seats, and that was announced. Mason was in the driver's seat and I was in the passenger seat. Logan looked at each of us. He was wearing a distinct frown-smirk combo on his face as he said his piece.

Problem was, he'd been saying it since we left Boston, since we landed in California, and since we'd been in the rental and driving three hours past Fallen Crest.

It'd been said. It'd been heard.

We were now at the part where we wanted to murder my brother-in-law. Or, correction, where *I* wanted to murder my brother-in-law. Mason was stoic and driving. He was able to get in the zone and tune Logan out. Taylor was sitting in her chair, reading on her phone. She had the whole tuning-out thing too.

Not me. I was a mom, so somehow that meant I always had to be aware and alert, and now I was close to grinding my teeth and yelling for a Logan time-out.

Five minutes in the back, please.

Mason grunted. "Tough shit."

Nice. Maybe he wasn't so 'tuned out.'

I looked at Taylor. "Can you keep him under control?"

She glanced up from her phone. "You know the answer to that question. You've known him longer."

Touché.

"*I'm* not sleeping with him."

Taylor just laughed. "Shouldn't have said that. He's probably refraining from twenty different inappropriate jokes as I'm talking."

"*Ahem.*" Logan gave us both a look. "It's because I love both of you—in *different* ways—and respect both of you that I'm not touching that. But Sam..." Logan leveled me with an aggrieved look, his eyebrows raised. "Can you watch what you say? Old Logan would've been all over that one, and can you imagine the innuendos?" He gestured to himself, his face tight. "But I'm here. Being polite—"

"Sorry. I thought since you're older and in law school, you'd be more mature."

"It's like you don't know me at all." But he was grinning.

"Logan." Insert some assertive tone here. I had to make my point. "We got a babysitter for the weekend. I got permission for a full weekend off from my training. Your brother is on a much-needed vacation before football training starts, and I have been needing Heather time even though I saw her a few weeks ago."

I had a point. What was it? "So shut it, okay?"

That was my point.

"All I'm saying is that we were supposed to do the yacht. Nate and Matteo were up for it. Now suddenly we're doing a camping thing. I'm not clear on the why?"

Mason glanced into the rearview mirror. "It was Nate's idea. He said something about family research. What's your issue? You like camping."

"That's when we were young. We did stupid shit back then like. We're old now. If we go camping, I prefer it to be on things like yachts. Or we stay in a mega-mansion and our camping is napping by the pool. I like that type of camping."

Taylor frowned at him. "Babe."

He shot her a look, frowning slightly, but his face softened. He reached out, touching her leg. "It's nothing. I'll get over it."

Good.

That was settled.

Two minutes later, "But why is Channing's sister coming? She and her friends are in high school. Why the fuck do they want to hang out with us?"

Mason arched an eyebrow. "Technically, they graduated."

Logan rolled his eyes, but settled back in his chair. "All the more. They're the ones who should be pranking the local cops."

"Uh." Mason and I shared a look.

I grinned. "I don't think that's the history with Bren and police."

Logan sighed. "I know. I do, I just..."

"Say what's really the issue." Mason glared in the mirror at his brother. "There's a reason we named our kid after you. You're acting just like Maddie."

That shut Logan up.

"I object."

But not for long.

Taylor finally cracked. "Logan! Stop, okay?"

He turned her way. "There's no privacy out there. We'll be in tents. You can hear everything in tents—"

"That's why you're so pissed? I know you can be all sorts of quiet when you want to, like when Sam and Mas—"

His hand clamped over her mouth and he fought back a grin. "Um, honey? Let's not tell them about the one time I was silent, maybe?"

He removed his hand, his head inching back.

Taylor smirked at *him* this time. "The *one* time? There wasn't just one time."

I shook my head. "Shut up, shut up, shut up. I don't want to know."

Logan scowled. "I wasn't the one who was going to spill the details."

"And I'm tired of your bitching," I added. "We're in tents for the weekend. Fucking deal with it."

Mason laughed, slowing the SUV and easing into a gas station. "Sam's spoken. You piss my wife off, that's going to piss me off." He parked and turned back to glare at his brother. "Don't piss me off."

He pulled the keys from the ignition, still glaring at Logan, and then was out of the SUV.

I grabbed my bag. "Taylor, you want something?"

She looked at the gas station, biting her lip. "I'll come in. We have another hour's drive, right?"

"More than that, and why aren't y'all asking me what I want?"

I didn't respond, but Taylor gave him a soft smile. She leaned over, tapping his chin before giving him a quick kiss. "Because you've annoyed everybody. Be smart and splurge on booze for the weekend. They'll all love you." She nodded to the liquor store next to the gas station.

"That's my woman. It's like you know me."

I heard another kiss as I exited the car, but after a moment Taylor joined me.

We were halfway across the lot when Logan asked, "Mase, you want something?"

"Not candy-flavored condoms," Mason replied, sounding distracted.

Logan laughed, and I grinned.

"I don't want to know," Taylor said.

The bell above the door rang when we went inside, and I was pleased to find it cleaner than I thought it would be. The outside was made of old brick, and the sign was missing a couple letters, but the inside had been maintained. That meant they'd probably have clean bathrooms, and once inside, I was thrilled to see I was right because that's really all that mattered. Clean bathrooms.

Taylor took the stall next to me, and after we washed our hands, she hit the motion-detecting towel dispenser with her shoulder. It began unraveling. "Logan's not really upset about the tents."

I glanced over, taking one of the towels she ripped off and handed to me. "He's pissed about having silent sex all weekend."

She laughed, finishing with her towel and tossing it in the garbage. Tucking a strand of her hair behind her ear, she headed for the door and paused, waiting for me. We had similar body frames, though I was a bit more slender from my running. She had light brown hair while mine was black. "No. He's upset about the weirdness going on with Matteo right now. He's worried about having him around Mason, because you know."

Oh.

Well that made a lot more sense.

Matteo had recently been released from the Los Angeles football team. Mason was still going strong with his team. They asked for a contract extension after next year's season. Matteo reached out, hoping Mason would do him a solid, but that wasn't really how it worked and Matteo didn't seem to understand that.

Yeah. There was weirdness.

"Logan thinks he's going to have to choose a side?"

Taylor had started to leave the bathroom, but once in the hallway, she turned back to me. "That's not it. Logan will always choose Mason, but I think he's not used to these dynamics. Nate's gotten close to Matteo recently and Logan and Nate are now living together. I think there's just dynamics going that Logan's not used to handling."

That made sense too.

I was starting to feel bad about not being more patient.

～

WE WENT our separate ways in the store.

She was paying for some items a little later when I brought my own stash up to the counter.

"It'll be fine."

Taylor glanced at me after she paid, taking her bag. "I know. Logan's just griping. He'll settle down in a bit."

She moved to leave the store as Mason was coming in.

He glanced back, watching her go. *Oh yeah.* That told me everything right there. My husband was notorious for not giving a shit about anyone he didn't love, and while he was cordial with Taylor, and she was the girlfriend of Logan's he liked the most, they didn't really have a relationship.

Him looking at her as she left spoke volumes.

I sighed as he stepped up next to me, reaching to pay for what I'd put on the counter.

I said, "It's the Matteo thing."

Mason told the gas attendant which gas he was paying for. He said to me, "Logan told me."

After paying for my items and the gas, he took my bag and ushered me to the side.

People were coming in and out, but so far, no one recognized him.

Which was a miracle considering he had an athlete's build. Wide shoulders. Trim waist. Plus, his black hair and green eyes were always striking. Mason photographed well and there were more than a few fan accounts dedicated just to him on Instagram. But he was keeping his head down, trying to remain hidden among the people. That was part of why we were camping where we were. Heather said people up here were so busy with the tourists that they didn't people-watch much. They preferred being *plastic* (Heather's word) to the money customers and paying attention to their local loved ones. *"It'll be super easy for your man to be incognito up there,"* she'd told me. *"And trust me, Bren and her guys won't give two shits either. They know you guys, but as you already know, they don't give a fuck anyway."*

I turned toward Mason. "How are you feeling about Matteo coming? You haven't mentioned it at all."

He eased us to the side, away from people going in and out of the station and put his hand on my hip. He glanced down, observing me. "Matteo knows I have no say over what a GM decides, or a coach, or even agents and managers. If I would've gotten asked my opinion, of course I would've said something for him, but I wasn't. I'm too new myself to throw my weight around. Plus, he's going to get picked up. He's too good not to. He just needs to wait it out a bit."

"Yeah."

Still, I felt the tension from him. I should've thought about this long ago. That was on me, not being a thoughtful wife. I gripped his shirt and bent to rest my forehead against his chest.

His hand smoothed down my back, and he drew me to him, hugging me closer.

"This is nice."

I laughed, tipping my head up to look at my husband.

He grinned down at me, his eyes concerned. He trailed a finger down the side of my face, his thumb grazing over my mouth. "You're tired. Don't stress about this. Please. It's not that big of a deal."

Yes. I was tired.

I was exhausted.

And now, gazing up at my husband, I was starting to lament why we hadn't gotten private campers for everyone. Silent sex wasn't sounding too good.

I had a new understanding for Logan.

"When are they arriving?"

Mason's hand slid up to the back of my shoulders. "Nate's been in Fallen Crest because of his family, so he and Matteo are driving up with Channing's sister and her crew."

Now that had me laughing. "Nate and Matteo with those four."

"Yeah." Mason's hand slid to the back of my neck, his lips lowering to mine. "I want you to have fun this weekend. Ignore Logan. Don't worry about Matteo or me, and enjoy time with Heather when she gets here. Okay?"

He closed the distance and his lips felt so good against mine.

Pleasure and lust began to warm me, and I melted into him as he cupped the side of my face. His thumb caressed over my cheek. "That's the whole point of this weekend—for *you* to have fun."

I pressed up, my lips nipping his before I stepped back. "And for you to have time with your man too."

He barked out a laugh. "I'll tell Logan you said that. He's going to gripe about Channing the rest of the way."

I groaned and took the bag of food from him. "I'll see you out there."

He nodded before heading to the back.

2

SAMANTHA

Two hours later and we were there. I could see why Heather said we wouldn't be bothered, because we were so far back in the woods I wondered if there was even internet. I knew that wasn't rational, but seriously—we were in the *back* backwoods somewhere. Thank goodness for GPS because that's the only way we found the camping site.

A sign finally appeared, proclaiming that we'd arrived at Broken Hills Resort.

Logan had a good chuckle at that name. I did not ask why, and Taylor hushed him when he tried to whisper something to her. Mason pulled up to a storefront that looked like it doubled as the check-in spot too. It was a little larger than a regular cabin, with log siding.

A bell jingled as we went through the door, and inside were several taxidermied animals, including a stuffed bear on its hind legs that gave me flashbacks of *Harry and the Hendersons*.

Mason paused when he saw the bear, glanced at me, and shook his head.

An older woman popped her head out from an office. When

she saw us, she smiled widely and rolled out from the office in her chair. When she reached the counter, she grabbed a hold and heaved herself up. She smoothed a hand over her unruly gray hair. Nothing stayed in place, but she moved on to adjusting her glasses on the bridge of her nose. She was a little heavyset and wore a beach cover-up over her clothes. It was bright pink, and grabbing one of the ends, she tucked it better around her waist and leaned over the counter.

"You must be the famous football star."

Logan started laughing. "Way to go incognito."

The lady had begun looking up some files, but she paused and lifted her head to frown at Logan. "Oh, we don't pay no mind to who is who out here." She found what she was looking for, pulled out a piece of paper, and went to the computer. "I just know we got a call asking if anyone here cared about football, and I said 'No siree, sweetie.'" She looked back at Logan, seeming to think he was the football star. "I don't know much about football, but I know you're a bit small for the game. Maybe a safety, hmm? Long eyelashes." She looked over at Mason. "You two brothers? You got the same lashes. You're a bit leaner than him. He's got those dark locks and you got more brown hair. And him, he's got the size. Both pretty, though. But anyhoo, we're a *real* football-following family here. Arsenal fans, if you get my drift. So y'all don't have to get your panties in a bunch and think we'll be selling your pictures to the *Gossip Moon*."

Logan was speechless for a second. "How do you know we weren't talking about real football?" He raised an eyebrow. "What if I'm an international soccer star that doesn't play for Arsenal?"

"Honey." She was *so* not impressed as she went to the printer. "You ain't no soccer star. We follow rising boys coming up when they're twelve in the clubs. You got me?" Not missing a beat, she slid the paper over in front of Mason and placed a pen beside it. "The call came in from a Heather Jax. She described you, said you could sign for the second campsite." She waved at us. "You all got an adjoining site with hers, and you can hitch up a camper or do tents." She pointed to a line. "Just sign there, and here's your map for the facilities."

Mason signed and took the map.

She slid another couple copies to me, winking. "For you and the women folk, since none of us were blessed with a stick we can pull out and aim."

Taylor laughed behind me. "I love her."

Logan patted Taylor on the arm and said under his breath, "She doesn't think I'm a soccer star."

Taylor laughed harder. "I know."

The lady overheard and pushed her glasses up to her forehead. She winked at Taylor. "Honey, he can pass for one. I just know he ain't." She looked him up and down. "You got the looks, all right—all smoldering and pretty-boyish. I know my players. This guy, I can tell, is the real football guy. He's quiet and hoping I won't take notice." She smiled at Mason. "You don't got nothing to fear from me."

Mason nodded. "Not really giving one shit either way, ma'am." Picking up the last two maps, he turned. "Let's go."

And we were off.

I glanced back and noted the lady's gaze had remained on Mason's ass until the door closed behind us.

We climbed back into the SUV and Taylor announced, "She had spunk."

Logan said, "She was okay."

We all laughed at that.

3

SAMANTHA

The campsite was gorgeous—a clearing between massive redwood trees, with our own path leading to a beach. The water was sparkling and the sand so fine it was surreal. But the biggest surprise wasn't the location or that as the lady had explained. There was another campsite right next to us. A path connected the two, with enough trees in between for privacy. The big shock was the three massive campers already in place next door, along with two others on the side.

"What the fuck?" Logan yelled.

Mason shared a look with me, a grin tugging at his mouth. "They got here fast."

I grunted, "No doubt."

The door opened on one of the campers and out walked Nate.

And walking wasn't the best way to describe Nate. He strutted his way down the three steps, grinning wildly at us, and Matteo popped out right behind him. Nate always reminded me of Mason, since both were similar height and both had black hair. But over the years, Mason's body had become more sculpted. It was a result from his job so maybe that was why Nate's face seemed a bit more fuller than Mason's chiseled jawline. Matteo was an inch shorter, more muscular than both Nate and Mason. He was proud of his Hawaiian ethnicity, but he seemed tanner than normal.

"Hell yeah!" Logan yelled. He was around the SUV in a flash, and the three guys were hugging and pounding each other's backs.

Taylor sighed. "SBCers, all three of them." She got out, but trailed behind at a slower pace.

Soul brotha connections.

Mason and I hung back.

I was in the twilight zone.

Mason should've been over there, hugging, pounding on the backs. Grins all around. He wasn't. I knew this had nothing to do with Logan and Nate. Both guys were at our house constantly. Nate had recently been traveling more to Fallen Crest. There were issues going on with his family, so he and Mason had started calling each other more, but it was Matteo.

And guy tension was the worst tension there was.

Matteo hadn't reached out to Mason. Mason *had* reached out, but was shut down so he didn't call again. Matteo was close to Nate, so it wasn't the issue where Matteo was talking shit about Mason. Nate and Logan would never stand for that, but the issue was that no one was talking about it.

It was felt. It was there. And the guys weren't sure how to handle it.

Old Mason would rip into Matteo, but we'd been busy. We were across the country. Marriage. Careers. Our little Maddie. So, life happened and I was sure life was happening for Matteo too.

Matteo was a good guy. Always had been, but yeah, things were just weird right now.

I was almost hoping a fight would just handle this and everyone could go back to being normal.

Mason let out a sigh. "Logan's pissed at me because I'm close to Channing."

"Logan loves Channing."

He shook his head. "But he's pissed at how close I've gotten with Channing too."

There was really nothing to say to that.

"And I don't want to fight Matteo," he added.

He must've been on the same brainwave as me?

Another breath of pain sliced through me for my man, but I ignored it. "Matteo will get over it too. It's painful for him now, but it won't be later."

"Nate used to be my best friend, but he's Logan's now."

These guys.

It'd been Mason and Nate. Nate left. Then it was Mason and Logan. Brothers. Then Nate came back, and I'd been in there instead of him. He'd been on the outskirts for the last few years, until Mason grew more serious about football. That meant more responsibilities, more pressure, more of a spotlight on him all the time. Nate didn't get that spotlight. Neither did Logan. It wasn't the same as when they'd grown up.

Mason had married me.

Mason had married his career.

And both Logan and Nate were in their own journeys.

They were in a different stage of life. It was just that simple.

But then there was Channing, who was in a different stage of his life altogether.

I knew my man was hurting, but I also knew only time would heal it.

"Hey." I reached for his hand, sliding my fingers through his and lifting both our hands so I could kiss his. I smiled, resting the side of my face against our hands. "It will be fine. Having friends, being loved is never a problem. Fighting to *keep* the love is the challenge, and we all know you dominate when you've been given a challenge."

His eyes grew dark, and his smile turned wolfish. "I love you." His gaze fell to my mouth. "And I want to drive out of here, find somewhere private, and bend you over in front of me." He leaned over, his other hand sliding around my neck. "Right now." And then his mouth was on mine, and the world melted away.

We took a little time to ourselves in the SUV.

4

SAMANTHA

When we got out, Mason and I went around to the back of the SUV and began to grab the bags. Nate came across the campsite toward us.

"Hey, man."

He and Mason hugged.

I had to stop and pause because it was so natural for both of them. They'd been through a lot, but Nate moved toward his childhood best friend and Mason held up, waiting for him. Both knew what the other would do and it was striking me how much these guys had been through. Maybe it was because of the Matteo awkward dynamic that I was realizing how different this was feeling, how much I'd taken for granted Mason's close friends that were like brothers to him. He and Logan were brothers, but in a different way, so was Nate to them. Channing was in that group, and until today I would've put Matteo with them as well.

I still would. So that meant things needed to get hashed out at this campsite. Pronto.

Mason asked, "Things work out here?"

He was referring to the reason Nate had been in California a lot more lately.

Nate shrugged. "It's a work in progress. How about that?"

Mason jerked his head toward the campers. "No tents?"

Nate's smile was blinding, and instant. He seemed more at ease suddenly. "Trust me. Tent camping sucks. You'll be thanking me tonight when you're wrapped up with Sam and you've got some privacy." His smile turned rakish. "Plus, I knew Logan would be griping about tents. So yeah, we splurged. Each of us has our own. We were figuring Matteo and I would take one of these. You and Sam the other. Logan and Taylor in the third. How's that sound?"

"Sounds good." Mason looked at me. "You good with that?"

I grinned back. I was easy with anything, just wanted Mason and Heather.

And speaking of Heather, I heard a door close at the campsite next to us and looked over. Voices and shouts filled the air soon after, and I could see movement through the trees.

"Where the fuck are they?"

Heather.

A pissed Heather.

Still sultry. Her hair was still a dirty blonde mess, but those smoky eyes that she sometimes made-up wasn't on her face. Didn't matter, though. Not for Heather. If she was standing, how she was now, she still oozed sex appeal.

God, I missed her.

Mason and Nate started laughing.

I was moving toward her before I realized what I was doing.

Mason called after me, "Yeah. Sam. I'll get everything situat—"

I wasn't listening anymore. I loved my man, but I needed my Heather right now.

I darted down the path that connected the campsites.

There she was.

Standing just outside Channing's truck. Frowning—or more

scowling, with her hands on her hips and her blonde hair tossed back over her shoulders.

"What the fuck is going on here?" she yelled. "I called. I explained the situation. We were supposed to get prime campin—" She saw me, and her voice stopped. A strangled sound came out next. "Holy fuck!"

Heather shrieked and ran to me.

I ran to her.

It was all glorious, with our hair in the wind and then our bodies hitting each other, and we didn't care. We laughed and squeezed each other as hard as we could. Then I was cursing—no, she started cursing first and I followed.

"Your future sister-in-law's lost her marbles, Bren," I heard a voice call.

I turned to find the tallest guy in the group looking our way. Next to him was a shorter guy, a bit more squat, and he grinned as he checked me out.

"Damn. Forgot how hot Samantha Kade is." He didn't seem to care that I could hear him. He tipped his head up. "Respect, Mrs. Kade, but you're hot. You get hotter each year too. Each week since it wasn't long ago that we saw you."

"Z!" A bark came from the girl who stepped out from behind them.

Bren, Channing's sister.

The words *beautiful wolf* were the best to describe her—dark hair, dark eyes, and a thin frame. I had jet-black hair, but there was something feral in Bren that I'd never attained. When I thought about growing up, living with Analise, I sometimes wondered why I hadn't gotten what Bren had inside her. But from what Heather had shared, there'd been some serious dark moments in Bren's life.

Heather sighed. "Mama Malinda has taken Bren under her wing."

"Good." For some reason, that made my chest feel lighter.

When I looked at Heather, I could see her own concern for the girl. "She's got you. She's got Malinda. She's got Channing. She's going to be okay."

Heather drew in a ragged breath, blinking back a tear.

"God," she whispered. "I hope so. She's been through so much already." She shook her head. "She could kick our ass, Sam. Thank God we didn't grow up at the same time she did. If we tangled with her..." Heather whistled under her breath.

I hip-checked her. "Don't let Logan hear you say that. He'll take it as a challenge."

Heather groaned and angled her head to check out where I'd come from. "True." She stepped back, untangling our arms and folding hers over her chest. She looked at all the campers. "We caravanned up with Nate, and he told us about the campers, but damn. Wow."

"I know. Nice, huh?"

"Yeah."

I turned to look at the two campers on their site. "I'm assuming Bren's crew will stay in one and you and Channing in the other?"

Bren and her friends had disappeared. I saw two, but I knew there was a third somewhere. There was no way Bren would come without that third guy.

"That'll be four together. They'll be okay with that?"

Heather barked out an abrupt laugh. "Yeah." She patted my arm. "You really don't understand how tight that group is. You, Mason, and Logan are tight, but those guys..." She shook her head, her eyes rolling upward. "It's almost ridiculous at times. You'll see. And yes, they'll prefer it. If Bren and Cross want alone time, they'll disappear and then come back."

Cross. That was his name.

A second truck pulled in and parked behind the first. Channing waved from behind the wheel and hit the horn, flashing us a grin.

Instantly, Heather loosened up.

Oh yeah, my friend was happy. That made me happy.

Before Channing got out, a guy who could've been his younger brother stepped out from the passenger side.

He paused, looking at me, and *oh yeah*, I could see what Bren saw in him. He was young, but it didn't matter. The guy was gorgeous—dark blond hair, a scowl that probably made most of the girls want him, and he was tanned and lean like Channing.

Without saying a word to any of us, he took off.

Heather waved. "Nice seeing you too, Cross."

He didn't look back, just lifted an arm.

Channing came over. A tattooed arm rose and he raked his hand through his dark blond hair, which was shorter than the last time I saw him. It accentuated the model face Channing always got teased for having. He was frowning now. "He's in a mood. I picked him up from his dad's house, and holy shit, I thought Mason could brood. Mase has got nothing on that kid." His words were laced with fondness and amusement. "He needs time with his other half, if you know what I mean."

Channing turned to me. "Heya, Sam."

I chuckled. "Hi, Channing."

He caught me up in a hug, but it was brief and polite.

I was best friends with his other half, and he was close enough to be considered a best friend to mine, but Channing and I didn't have much of a relationship. We both loved our soulmates, and because of that, we were friendly. Anything else felt inappropriate, but a sort of respect had formed between us.

After he pulled Heather in for some brief Heather/Channing time, he went off to search for my man.

Heather craned her neck, looking toward our campsite. "Is Taylor over there too?"

I didn't have time to answer. Just as a bunch of male voices got loud and raucous, Taylor came walking our way from the path. She paused, looked back, and shook her head as she approached.

"Buddy!"

"Man!"

"Hell yeah!"

Cheers filled the air behind her.

Taylor came over, hugged Heather, and murmured, "I'm fairly certain there are going to be two groups tonight: the boys..." She indicated behind her. "And the women."

"And Bren's crew will be the third," Heather added.

Taylor frowned. "Who's Bren?"

5

SAMANTHA

Gender roles were reversed for this campout.
I had no idea how it happened, but I knew when it happened.

Logan had decreed that we needed better food. Not more food, *better* food, so off the guys went to the nearest grocery store. They were also tasked with stopping for more booze. (Not better booze, *more* booze this time.) And while they were at it, we put them in charge of picking up anything else miscellaneous we needed.

Bren asked for a knife.

I had no idea why, but Channing only stared her down before sighing. "Fine."

I asked for hand sanitizer and toilet paper (since none of the campers had any).

Taylor handed Logan a list. Knowing her, it included all the items everyone else needed but forgot to request.

Heather asked for cigarettes, and Channing was back to doing his stare-off. He didn't sigh this round.

Heather's the one who sighed, gritting her teeth. "Fine. Just whiskey."

The corner of Channing's mouth curved up, but he ran a tattooed hand over his face. "She quit this year and *still* keeps asking for a carton."

Heather lifted her shoulders in a helpless shrug. "What do you do? It's reflex. People ask if I need something, I need cigarettes. It's automatic."

So Matteo, Nate, Logan, Mason, and Channing all piled into an SUV and drove away with Mason behind the wheel. I should note that Matteo had not greeted Mason or myself. He stayed beside Nate and Logan, and when all the guys were together, Matteo was quiet. I knew this because I watched.

Before the football weirdness, Matteo would've come over to give me a hug.

There was no hug.

I noticed this. Taylor and Heather did not. Neither was close to Matteo, but I knew all of the guys had noticed. So I was mulling over that because I wasn't sure how I felt about it. Not that I had a say because Nate and Logan were friends with Matteo. He and Mason would be again, I was hoping, so that was my answer. I would be fine with it because everything would work out in the end.

Or I was hoping.

So the guys went shopping and the girls went to grab firewood.

I dropped my second load by the fire pit and glanced around.

Heather came up behind me, dumping her load.

"Where are your girl and her crew?"

She snorted. "Fuck if I know. Knowing them, we won't see them until Zellman decides he's hungry. Honest to God, that kid is the smallest of all of them and he eats the most."

I grinned at her. "Who's the tall one again?"

"Jordan. Cross is—"

"—the gorgeous broody one?"

She flashed me back a grin. "Yeah."

Taylor approached with her third haul. There were small beads of sweat on her forehead.

She wasn't alone. It was hot out and we all started to sweat a little.

I sighed, bending over. Locking my fingers, I raised my arms over my head, stretching. "I should go for a run."

Heather eyed me, her hand resting on her hip. "You've started training already, right?"

I straightened and brought my arm over my chest, stretching it to the left and right.

I reversed and did it the other way. "Yeah, but it's hard." Training was a full-time job, and leaving Maddie to do my long runs was a whole other issue. "My trainer has been pushing me hard, but I just want to stay and snuggle with Maddie."

Both Heather and Taylor softened.

"She's such a cutie." Taylor smiled.

I tensed, groaning. "You're making me want to go back and say screw it to this weekend."

Heather frowned. "Why don't you?"

Because...

I had to remember the reason myself. "Because I need friend time, and I do. I really do..." But my voice hitched into a wistful sigh. *Maddie.* Gah. Maddie. I could feel her body in my arms already, her weight, her smell. She would wiggle around, searching, and then she'd sniff my neck and collapse into one of her long sleeps.

I just wanted to play with her, pretend to eat her little toes and fingers.

And her shrieks—I could hear them in the air.

"I bet Malinda is having a grand time with her."

I shot Heather a grateful look. She was trying to make me feel better, and I nodded. "She was salivating over getting to keep her for the weekend, but I wanna go back now. I really wanna go back."

Both girls were laughing.

It was obvious I *wasn't* going to go back.

"Being a mom changes you." I hadn't known. I hadn't been prepared. "You think you're good and you got life going for you, and then bam. You have a little baby and everything tips upside down and your priorities totally change."

Not that my priorities really had changed.

I loved Mason.

I loved my family.

But it was more.

Maddie made me feel more, love more. She just made me more.

The girls understood. Both smiled gently at me, and then suddenly Heather declared, "I want to get drunk. I know you're having a mom moment, but I'm having a Heather moment and my moment is the reason we're here. To cut loose and have fun. Let's do a girls' night. Fuck the guys, I mean, you know."

Taylor was grinning, her eyes twinkling. "I'm for that. I love our girls' nights."

"Does this extend for our sleeping arrangements too?"

"We'll stay over here and crash where we crash."

Heather considered it and then nodded. "Yeah. Okay. I'm in."

Taylor's eyes got big. "The booze is on our side—the booze Logan already bought. I'm snagging as much as I can before they get back."

6

BREN

The guys were down at the beach, and they wanted a few things: a bottle of Jack, a couple blankets, and a lighter. I volunteered to come back to get them because I knew this crowd the best. That said, though, I didn't really know them that well.

I knew Heather. Loved Heather.

I knew Channing. Loved my brother. Obviously.

But the rest, I'd only met them once or twice, seen them a few other times, but they all left me with different vibes. I was okay with Sam and Mason the most, and that was me being lenient with that word.

I didn't adult well.

That wasn't meaning me *being* an adult.

That was me meaning I didn't like adults.

Logan, I didn't know about him. He was wild and unpredictable. He had a lot simmering under the surface, and I could literally see the anger there. He wanted to let it out, but he wasn't because he was an adult. Adults couldn't just be. They had to suppress, and that Logan dude was tired of suppressing. He had shit to say, so I was hoping the liquor they were buying would tip the balance and he'd erupt. That shit would be fun to watch.

As for the rest:

Nate, my opinion was being held in check with him. He seemed like a whole 'stay tuned' issue.

Matteo, I didn't know his problem. He seemed nice, but something was going on with him. I didn't like it and my read was to steer clear of him, and again, I had no reason why I was picking that read from him. I just was.

As for the other girl, Taylor. I liked her.

I might not like adults much, but I could read adults. I read them really well, and I was reading that Taylor was in a mass amount of pain. She was nice and lovely on the surface, but there was stuff inside her. Stuff that people either weren't feeling or stuff that she hid well, like *extremely* well. Even her man, the wild suppressing one didn't seem to be checking in with her. He was all up in his head, doing his thing and leaving his woman to do her thing, but after watching her a little, I saw that was her thing.

She flew under the radar because that's what she wanted.

She didn't get her due credit.

I was giving her the due credit because I liked her. I almost liked her more than Heather's best friend. I mean, if I was going to be put in an apocalyptic situation where I had to choose who to be quarantined with? I'd choose Taylor over everyone else.

Huh.

I surprised myself with that answer, but then I tuned back into their conversation.

I was standing behind our camper and the girls had all decided to get rip-roaring drunk (not their words, but I was paraphrasing because I could tell that was their meaning) and I was rethinking our whole plan for the night.

Forget about grabbing the supplies, I went back to get the guys.

We had a whole show that was going to stream live and in person for us tonight.

7

SAMANTHA

We were drunk by the time Mason and the guys got back. I had no clue why they'd taken so long, but bottoms up. Mason came toward our campfire, and I greeted him by lifting my drink and yelling, "Ninja Sam is baaaaack, honey!"

He stopped, ran a hand over his face, and looked down. "Christ. You're wasted."

"I'm so fucking wasted." A thought came into my head, and I scrambled over to him, pulling my phone out with the hand that had the drink in it. "Hey! You have to look."

He caught my drink just as Heather started to say something.

Then he reached into my pocket and pulled my phone out himself. "Okay. What am I looking for?"

"There are pictures. Malinda sent Maddie pictures, and she's so cute!"

I'd been staring at them for the last twenty minutes, and according to Heather, I'd shown them to her five different times. All five of them. And the texts Malinda was sending me.

"How long were we gone for you to get this smashed?" Mason

was grumbling at the same time he was scrolling through my phone. "Why is Malinda giving you hourly updates?"

"Because I asked for thirty-minute updates, and she refused to do that."

He lifted heavy eyes to me. "Sam."

I tried to mimic him, but that meant I had to stick my bottom lip out too. "Mase."

"You don't need hourly updates from Malinda."

"Yes, I do." Because I did.

So did he.

And if he didn't want them, I'd get them for him.

Because that's who I was now. A mom. A mother. I had another entire being dependent on me. She'd been made from my loins. I pushed her out of my body. She was me, made from me, and it was my job—

"Stop." His hand came down over my forehead.

"Wha—" I smacked it off. "What are you doing?"

"Stopping the thoughts. I can literally see them. You are fine. Maddie is fine. You pumped enough milk for her, and it's frozen, and everything is okay. Malinda got the thirty-page write-up on what to do if any scenario happens while we're gone. And it's one night."

God. One night.

I wasn't going to last.

His hands came to my shoulders, and he peered down. "Babe."

Ooh. That sounded nice. I moved into him, but wait... I had a drink.

I looked around. Where'd that drink go?

"Samantha." He tugged me against him. My body next to his...oooh, his very fine and very strong and very athletic—my husband was hot. He just got better looking as he got older too, and being a pro athlete, he could go all freaking night. And his thighs? His thighs were Thor thighs. They were god thighs.

My hands fell to them, and I squeezed.

They were *my* thighs.

I loved those thighs, and especially when he was pumping into me—

His hand came down over my mouth this time.

"Hhhmph!" I slapped his hand away again, scowling. "What was that for?"

Heather drawled behind me, "Girl, those weren't thoughts you were keeping to yourself."

"Wha—" I turned to her, eyebrows up in horror. "I didn't."

She gave me a resigned nod. "You were. And while I was entertained, especially with the Thor thighs, we don't need to know what it's like to have your hot pro NFL guy pumping into you. Nope. Not a visual we need."

Taylor stood next to Heather, holding her drink—and mine! I reached out for it.

She handed it to me and nodded. An emotion flashed in her eyes, and she turned to Mason. "We're doing girls' night. Guys have to stay over there."

"Fuck," he responded. His eyes narrowed, and he looked carefully at each of us. "Do I want to know what brought this on?"

"No. We're good." Heather tugged me back, lifting her chin in the direction he'd come. "I got both of these handled, but we're doing girls' night over here. Channing got the text. He's bunking with you. Put him on the couch. I don't care, but Logan is not to be over here. He's going to be the one to push it."

He sighed. "Shit."

"Shit is right!" Taylor pumped her arm, her drink sloshing over.

I had a moment of clarity.

Heather and I, we'd gone through hell and heaven, parties and blackmailing. There'd been slight stalker issues. Crap. There'd just been a ton of shit we'd gone through—Mason too—

and here we were. Still together. Still friends. And still having a good time. A damn good time.

My phone pinged, and I went to grab it.

I have a baby! Did I tell you all that already? A baby!

She was adorable. Big fat cheeks. Green eyes like her daddy's. She had my hair. I mean, we both had black hair, but it was mine on her head. I just knew it. And she was going to be a runner. I could already tell. She was always pumping her little feet and hands in the air. Her little eyebrows would flatten, and she'd scowl and wave those limbs until she was exhausted. Just like me.

I was already proud.

But Mason wasn't having it right now. He raised my phone up and moved back, blocking me with his hip. He wrapped his other hand around my waist.

"I'll get the updates, okay?" he said. "Maddie is fine, but maybe I want to see the pictures. Hmmm?"

I reached for the phone again.

Heather wrapped an arm around my waist, holding me back.

She smiled sweetly at Mason, and I know she was smiling sweetly even though I wasn't looking at her because I could *hear* it. I could feel it. She said, "We're good. Thank you for being in charge of the Maddie updates, because while I love my little goddaughter, hourly reports are something I can catch up on tomorrow all at once, if you know what I mean."

Mason's lip twitched. "I'm getting your drift."

"Good, good." She nodded. "You guys have a nice night."

His eyes skirted over us before he seemed to come to some decision. "Okay." He pressed his lips to my forehead and skimmed his hand down my arm to mine. "Have fun, okay?"

A tingle of sensations trailed his touch, or wait...trail of tingles? Yeah. That made more sense. I tipped my head up, he dropped his mouth back to mine for a moment, and then he was gone, leaving me in a rush of desire, warmth, and tingling extremities.

I waved my hand in front of me, fanning myself. "Do you all appreciate the fineness of my man?"

Heather gave me a blank stare.

Taylor's eyes were wide.

Heather's hand was still over her mouth.

Right. I put my hands in my back pockets. "Never mind. Wipe that from the transcript."

Heather snorted. "I changed my mind."

Both Taylor and I looked at her.

"I'm not going to wrangle you guys or monitor you. I'm getting drunk too." She let go of Taylor. Taking three steps, she bent and grabbed the bottle of whiskey. She pushed off the cap and tipped her head back, taking three shots in one large gulp.

WE WERE LEAPFROGGING.

I didn't know why.

I didn't know how.

I didn't know who started it, but we were leapfrogging.

Heather jumped over me.

I jumped over Taylor.

Taylor went over Heather.

But wait.

None of us had ribbitted, or croaked, or whatever sound frogs make.

Ribbit.

We had to do it all over again.

And we were supposed to go somewhere. There'd been a point to this... Anyway, off we went.

Ribbit. Heather leapt over me.

Ribbit. I leapt over Taylor.

Ribbit! Taylor over Heather.

Now we were in Heather's camper.

Taylor had been in the bathroom, but now she was coming back. She had a funny expression on her face, but I was almost too far gone to notice because I was crying.

I didn't know why I was crying, but I was crying.

Oh!

"I miss Maddie so much."

Taylor moved around us, crawling back up onto the bed. "Sorry, guys."

Heather's arms were around me, and then a hand was slapping my forehead.

I looked up. It was Taylor, but it wasn't her hand. It was her foot. Her head was twisted the other way in the bed, her arm up and covering her eyes. "Guys."

We both looked up.

Taylor shook her head. "Never mind. I'm sorry, Sam. You miss your little girl."

"My baby. I'm a horrible mother. I left her—"

Taylor groaned, sitting up. She took her foot away. I kinda liked having it there. Propping herself up, her hands on the bed, she frowned at me. "It's one night, Sam. You're going to see her tomorrow, and we're all going to Manny's tomorrow night."

She was right.

That was right.

I'd see my baby tomorrow.

But right now I was missing her, missing her weight in my arms, missing her little smell, her little sounds, even her crying.

"I'm okay, right?" I was so drunk. "Or am I going to scar her for life that I left for tonight?"

Heather cursed, her head moving from my shoulder. She looked exhausted, bags under her eyes. "Girl, get it together. One freaking night, and you gotta do it now. You'll have other bonding times and breastfeeding times later. This is the time when you can get a night away, and you're due one night—if anything, for your sanity."

Taylor lay back down but threw up her arm. "But not ours, because holy hell, Samantha, you are annoying right now."

That got through.

Taylor had called me annoying, and I knew Heather was irked.

I sighed. "Remember the days when I was Ninja Sam? Now I'm just Crying Mom Sam."

They both laughed.

"Fuck's sake. We're all just getting old. Come on." Heather had had enough.

Of what I didn't know yet, but she snagged my hand and pulled me to my feet. She reached for the door.

Taylor slid down from the bed. "Where are we going?"

Heather led the way out and down the stairs. "I'm bored."

"Oh no."

That was me, but I didn't pause.

I didn't have a good feeling about where Heather was going. I saw the look that flashed over her face before she got up. A bored Heather wasn't good. She had a tendency to be like Logan in that respect.

She turned around, walking backwards now. "Taylor." She gave her a serious look. "I'm apologizing ahead of time."

"For what?" Taylor's voice went up a notch.

I shook my head. I knew Heather. I knew that look.

This wasn't going to be good.

Oh no.

Oh no.

Oh no.

She was heading down the path. It was *the* path—the path we weren't supposed to walk tonight. We'd set the perimeters. We'd drawn the line. We'd declared our mission. It was girls' night. We were supposed to be rallying around Taylor, and Heather was going to bomb that all away.

I raised a hand. "Can we go back to leapfrogging?"

Heather ignored me, saying to Taylor, "You're drunk. I'm drunk. Everyone's drunk."

"Heather, no." I tried again.

"What are you doing, Heather?" Taylor asked.

A smirk came over Heather's face, and that was so bad, so very bad.

"You didn't say anything, but don't think I didn't notice."

Oh no.

"Heather..."

But she was gone. She was talking, and she wasn't going to stop.

She kept walking as she did, "He was with Nate. He greeted Logan. Didn't greet you. Didn't greet me. Didn't even look at Taylor. And when Mason was over there, he didn't say a word. I was watching. You don't think I was, but I was. My life, who we roll with now, you have to have eyes everywhere. I have eyes everywhere, and I noticed." She stopped, looking at me. "Drunk time is the best therapy time. Matteo's going to get some therapy."

"Tonight?" Taylor whispered, and even in the dark I could see the blood drain from her face.

"Tonight. I got the feeling."

Heather nodded and turned back around, marching over the path.

Taylor came up beside me. "She has a feeling?"

I nodded. Yep. I knew that feeling.

Heather was about to raise holy hell, and she was doing it to help Mason? I wasn't sure.

"Oh boy." That's all I said as I grabbed Taylor's hand and followed Heather.

We could've gone back, but neither of us considered that option. I think we both wanted to have this out too.

Then Heather was at the other campfire. "Matteo, you're doing the empty chair."

Taylor looked at me again, but I was right there with her.

The empty chair?

8

BREN

T he plan had been to go easy on the alcohol tonight, since there were adults with us.

That'd been the plan.

What we were doing instead was each of us was fisting our own hard liquor bottle. Each had a cup with a mixer in there, but for the most part, we were drinking straight up.

Oh well.

None of us really cared; we were avidly listening to these women as we were sitting behind Heather's camper.

They were loud as fuck, even being inside the camper. We could've been in our camper and still heard their shrieks—not to mention the leapfrogging. Jordan and Zellman had thought that was so funny, Cross had to stuff their own shirts in their mouths.

Though we hadn't really needed to worry about Heather and her friends hearing us, since they were blasted.

Zellman whispered, "This is like live MTV shit."

Jordan grinned. "Adults get on our asses for acting like this now, but fuck. We can do this same shit at their age? I'm in. Forget the stupid crew rules."

I frowned.

Cross looked at him, leaning around me. "That makes no sense."

Jordan paused, lifted his bottle, and shrugged. "It made sense in my head."

Zellman just giggled. He'd been all about the giggling tonight. "I want to get laid." He looked at me. "Can we call our girls?"

Cross answered for me, "No."

"Why not?" He indicated to me with his bottle. "You got yours here."

"We ain't doing shit right now. This is a crew weekend."

Jordan snorted.

Zellman laughed, holding his bottle in the air toward the camper. "Like you and Bren won't slip away when we're way past trashed, but whatever. It's cool. I get it. Crew weekend with some free live entertainment. And I think the chicks left."

"What?"

Fuck. He was right. It was silent inside their camper.

Cross patted my hip, and I led the way.

One by one, we stood and crept out, each still holding our bottle. I couldn't imagine what we looked like, but we hurried, like bonfire creepers, around the campfire, and instead of following them down the obvious path, I cut across toward the beach area. There was a thinning in the trees down here, one I knew the adults hadn't taken the time to find.

I moved forward until we had crossed the beach access of their campsite too. We went to the far side of their site, moving up through the next campsite, which was empty, and entered a clearing in the woods. There was enough room to sit, but that wasn't enough.

Handing over their booze, Cross and Jordan went back. After a moment they returned, carrying an entire picnic table. They placed it in the pathway that would've connected the Kades' campsite to the empty site behind us. Setting it just beyond where any light might shine over us, each of us climbed up.

Butts on the table, feet where we would've normally sat, we hunkered down for another front row seat to whatever was about to unfold.

Cross leaned close, resting his hand behind me and his mouth came to my ear. "Z's not wrong. I'm going to want to slip away later."

A shiver of anticipation ran through me, and I nodded. "I know."

I turned my head, just slightly, and felt his lips there.

I closed my eyes, inhaling, savoring this moment.

Then his mouth moved and his lips applied pressure.

Tingles spread through me, and a full-on shiver went down my spine.

I leaned forward, and we were silently making out.

Then Jordan coughed. "Not fair."

Zellman answered, right next to him, "Exactly."

Cross chuckled and left another nip against my lips before he moved away. "Fuck off, you two."

They both started laughing, but silently.

Then we tuned in, because shit was getting good over there.

9

SAMANTHA

This was happening.

I didn't want it to happen, but it was happening.

Taylor groaned, shrinking into my side as much as she could, but we were here. Heather was wading in, and we were backing her up—even though in this situation Heather was really just lighting the bomb and tossing it into the group. The bomb wasn't even hers to throw, but she was doing it, and if I hadn't acknowledged it before, I definitely had a girl crush on Heather.

She stepped up to where the guys had formed a semicircle around the fire pit. Her legs set wide, her hand went to her hip. The other held her whiskey bottle, because we'd taken to just passing the bottle around.

"Heather!" Taylor hissed.

She ignored her. "Matteo." She found him, frozen mid-sip of his own bourbon.

He looked at each of us before returning to Heather.

"What's the deal?" she asked. "Sam hasn't said anything, but I can tell. You're being awkward. You're setting off awkward vibes. What gives?"

He made a startled choking sound.

I'd never seen Matteo shocked before. I was seeing it now, and I almost wished I could take a picture of it. I didn't think I'd ever see it again.

Could I?

I was trying to remember... Where was my phone?

I patted my pockets. It wasn't in there.

Mason suddenly half-snorted a laugh, his head looking down. His shoulders shook.

I frowned.

Wait. Did he have my phone?

Then Heather clued in, frowning at Mason and then me, and her eyebrows pinched together. She wasn't cluing in all the way. "I don't want to ask, but I'll ask you instead. What's up Matteo's ass?"

"Heather." Channing stood.

She shot a hand out in his direction. "No. In some ways, this is my crew. You have your crew, Chan, and you're all up in their business and taking care of them. This is me doing that for my group. I know something's going on and I don't like it. I've never felt this weird shit before and I've been around these guys. We've gone through some dark moments before. This, though. This has my skin crawling."

I shot Logan a look. He and Nate.

Both were looking away, and both had their jaws clenched.

Interesting.

Then, as if knowing he was cornered, Matteo let out an audible sigh.

He was empty chairing. I think? I still wasn't sure what that meant, and I feel like I should know. Like, I feel like it's something that I should know and I was feeling like a dumbass for not knowing.

Another thing I could use my phone for. I could google that and then be in the know.

"Sam." Mason's voice was coming out strangled. "Honey."

Oh no.

I recognized that one, and I was having déjà vu. Not a good déjà vu too.

I looked at Heather. "I'm talking out loud, aren't I?"

She hid a grin, biting down on her lip. "You do tend to be hilarious when you drink so you're not saying a word. You keep on thinking whatever you're thinking."

Someone else started snorting/laughing, but I scanned the group.

I didn't think it was coming from any of them. That was weird.

"Matteo." Heather coughed in a not subtle way at all. "You're up."

He was doing the empty chair thing now.

His eyes flashed at Heather and his mouth tightened. "I don't know what you want me to say, Jax."

She retorted, "Whatever's going on."

"Whatever's going on?" His mouth flattened and his jaw clenched. He was in *that* club. His shoulders got all rigid as well. "Fine. Fuck it. What's going on is that I got released from my team, which I get. It happens, but they reached out to Mason's team and offered to trade me. They didn't take me. Mason had an opportunity to vouch for me, since we're friends and all, but he didn't."

"That's not how it works."

Matteo glared at him. "That's exactly how it works."

"They didn't ask me."

"Bullshit."

"It's not, man. And that team doesn't run like that."

Matteo was quiet.

I saw Logan and Nate sharing a look, but both remained quiet.

"You know that team doesn't work like that. Some guys have sway, but not me. I'm too new. No way in hell would they ask. If they had asked me, I would've vouched for you. I didn't even know about it until it was done and you were released. You're the one who told me about it. I got that text from you and it was fucked up."

I also needed to note this.

This was the most not-heated argument Mason had ever been in, that I'd witnessed.

He'd been in plenty. Fisticuffs. Fighting words. Cops showed. All that happened and it had gotten bad at other times, but this time, he wasn't that angry. He was hurt, but that was surprising me too. He was letting it be heard that he was hurt. He wasn't standing or throwing out threats or trying to shut someone up like that. All past Mason fights.

This Mason fight, I didn't even want popcorn to watch it.

It was very anticlimactic.

"Samantha." A hand clasped on my arm.

I looked. Taylor was there, biting the inside of her cheek. She drew me closer and whispered, "Maybe we can try to not share everything?"

"Oh." I clamped a hand over my mouth, then said, "Ididnt-knowiwasdoingit."

Crap.

Double crap.

Heather was shaking her head. Taylor was trying not to laugh.

Channing was outright watching me, enjoying everything.

Mason seemed frustrated.

I touched my lips, making sure they weren't moving. They weren't. Thank goodness.

I think I'll just keep my finger right here, just at the corner, and make sure they aren't moving anymore.

Yes, indeed. I'll just do that.

And I waited. No weird looks.

I think I had a handle on it now.

Mason was saying, "...and I have to also say that after you texted me, I did ask for a meet. They sent a guy down and got my opinion. I told them you're a good player and they'd be idiots not to take you. After that, I really can't do anything."

Matteo was still watching Mason, but his glaring had faded.

Then he sucked in some air.

His cheeks emptied out and he looked down. His hands clasped each other in his lap and I heard the word, "Fuck," whispered from him. "*Fuck!*"

He swung that accusing look to Nate and Logan. "You guys know this?"

Both shook their heads.

Nate said, "You asked us not to say anything. We didn't."

Mason's jaw clenched. Now he was a member too.

Matteo swung his head Mason's way. "And knowing you, you probably didn't offer anything?"

"You're in the family. I was waiting for you to come to me." A beat. "You never came to me."

"Shit." It was low and swift, and Matteo's hands were in fists beside his legs now. "Goddamn."

Logan spoke up quietly, "When Mason and I fight, we usually handle it right away. I can't help it. I can't keep shit in. And he and Nate, that shit gets hashed out between them too. I mean, yeah, there's spillage to our group sometimes but not all the time. We're all older too." His gaze went to his brother, then returning to Matteo. "Seems a conversation is the way to go now. Don't you think?"

Matteo flinched.

The message was sent.

In his way, Logan had tried to be Matteo's friend, but he was also showing that he was on Mason's side and had been on Mason's side this whole time.

Matteo lifted his head again. His eyes were almost searing from regret. "What do I do now? How do I make this up? I feel like I hurt you and that was never my intent. I was stupid. Dumb.

I should've called and I didn't. Pride, man. You know? It's a bad fucker."

I almost let out a sound of annoyance, because this really was a letdown. A few words, a brief moment of tension, and now the apologies were flying? There wasn't even a swear word—

wait. There had been.

Nevermind.

There'd been swearing, but no raised voices. No beer bottles were thrown or used as a weapon. I'd heard about Channing's recent showdown. There were no motorcycles roaring through the bonfire.

No guns. (Not that there really ever had been. I didn't think...)

Wasted Old Sam was just that, wasted and old. My memory was slipping already.

I'd have dementia by the time Maddie was twenty.

Oh God! That couldn't happen.

I couldn't forget my baby.

"Sam. Okay."

My finger had slipped. I already knew when Heather linked her arm through mine. "Maybe we should." But she paused and looked at Taylor. "Is girls' night over?"

Taylor was yawning.

I snorted. That was the answer.

Heather seemed to deflate all in one go. "Okay. I'm a little tired. I don't know if I'll be able to walk tomorrow."

And at that moment, Channing had been frowning at Heather's legs. He spoke up, "Babe, why are your knees all dirty?"

Taylor started laughing.

I started snickering.

Heather shot us both a dirty look before saying to Channing, "Not because of why you're thinking."

Taylor offered, "There was leapfrogging."

Silence. From all the guys.

All eyes turned our way.

"Leapfrogging?" Logan's eyebrow raised, just one of them. His head inclined forward at a slight angle. "You were leapfrogging, Firecracker?"

She flushed, but a soft smile was on her face. "Yes. And it was fun."

Channing asked, his tone more guarded, "Heather. Leapfrogging?"

If I didn't see it, I wouldn't know it was possible, but Heather was flushing too.

And I didn't know why leapfrogging was so scandalous, unless they were thinking of—

oh.

Ohhhh.

I didn't think they were thinking of the actual leaping over part, more of the other part. The position part, and now I was flushing, and eyeing Mason, who was giving me a knowing smirk.

Yeah. Girls' night was over.

Mason came over, his hand sliding around my waist. He tugged me away from Taylor and into his chest. Bending his head, he asked in my ear, "You wanna try some leapfrogging in the camper tonight?"

"Yes, please."

I was refraining from a ribbit sound.

But I had to touch my lips to make sure they refrained too.

He stifled a laugh and wrapped his other arm around me. I slid my arms around him, and we took a moment, away from the tension and the disappointing drama. It was Mason and me. Mom and dad. Husband and wife, and even though we were with our family and friends, I needed this.

There was never a time I wouldn't want Mason to hug me.

He nuzzled into my neck, kissing my throat.

I shivered, and he whispered in my ear, "And by the way, because I heard a little bit, you are fine to have one night away. You are a great mom, Sam. You worry about her, and you love her,

but you are allowed one night off. And Malinda is allowed one
night to bask in being a grandma too."

Right.

We were doing this for Malinda.

I grinned, tipping my head back. His eyes got all dark and soul-
ful, and then his gaze moved to my mouth. He began to trace around
my mouth with his finger, and I felt a whole new slew of shivers.

He felt them too and grinned, his smile turning wolfish.
"Fuck, I love you."

"I love you too."

Heather groaned next to us, "I have to say, I love Channing
too. He is my soulmate in this wild and crazy ride we call life, but
you two are taking the trophy for being so fucking cheesy right
now." A second later, "And we lost another pair."

"What?" I pulled out of Mason's arms.

Taylor and Logan had gone over to stand in front of one of the
campers.

The fight was done.

I was assuming Mason and Matteo would be fine now, so he
and Nate had moved on to their next mission. They were taping
bottles of booze to their hands.

Channing approached and stepped up behind his woman.

He pulled her back to his chest and dipped his mouth to her
shoulder. She knew it was him, knew the second he got close, and
a whole different look came over her face, one that was molten
and wanting. As his lips touched her bare shoulder, her body
trembled. She gulped, her hand sliding around his head to cup
the back of his neck.

"Hey," she whispered to him.

"Hey," he whispered back, dropping another kiss to her
shoulder before lifting his head. He frowned, his eyes sweeping
around us. "Where's my sister?"

A sharpness sliced his words. His eyebrows pulled together.

"We're in the middle of nowhere. What are the odds those four got into some fight with someone?"

I noted that he didn't say those four had gotten into a fight amongst themselves. Nope. It was with someone *else*.

Heather muttered a curse and stepped free from his hold. Her eyes were alert, and she was scanning both campsites now, or scanning what she could see. "You're right. There's no way they wouldn't find drama somehow."

She began to stride forward, to the path connecting our campsites.

"Speak for yourself!" a voice hollered, and Channing's sister materialized from the woods opposite us.

She walked with confidence, her shoulders back, head up, and behind her the three guys followed. The golden model was at her backside, and the other two filtered out, snickering to each other. Each of them held a bottle of alcohol, and not one seemed ashamed of that fact.

Channing grunted, returning to Heather's back. His hand went to her hip. "You guys been there the whole time?" He was eyeing the alcohol. "You been drinking those the whole time too?"

Cross moved ahead, his arm grazing against Bren's. "We were wondering if we could join the party or not."

Again. I noted the lack of acknowledgement about the alcohol.

The other two had noticed what Nate and Matteo were doing. The shorter one hit the taller one, nodding to the guys, and soon they broke off, going over to them. "Are you guys doing fortyhands?"

Nate straightened up. "No, because that'd be dumb and immature, and Matteo and I are both adults. We're mature..."

The shorter one smirked. "So you're doing twentyhands?"

"Exactly. I'm going to have to piss in five minutes anyway."

Cross and Bren watched the exchange before returning to where they'd been hiding.

A second later, they came back carrying a picnic table. Their other two friends went over and helped bring it over to Nate and Matteo, and then the four climbed on and got comfortable.

Two of them sat on the bottom bench part, taking the tape from Matteo to stick their own bottles to their hands. The taller one offered the tape to Cross, who shook his head.

"Not a fucking chance, Jordan."

"We're not going to finish this. It'll make us sick, but for a while. You know?" Jordan grinned. "I was thinking we should have a crew circle tonight."

A slow grin appeared on Cross' face. "Yeah, maybe." He jerked his head up, indicating the rest of us. "But not in front of these people."

Jordan nodded.

Heather bit her lip, her eyes skating from Bren to Taylor and settling on me. "I thought there'd be fireworks tonight, and I'm not talking about the Fourth of July kind."

"I did too."

Channing leaned into her. "I'm thinking the *married* couples are going to be turning in soon." His eyes were on Logan, who had pulled Taylor into their camper.

We could hear their raised voices, though we couldn't make out the words, and then the camper started rocking.

Well. Goodnight, then.

Mason shook his head.

Channing started chuckling.

A moan came from inside the camper, and that was loud enough that everyone else heard it. Conversation stopped on the other side of the campfire, and Jordan pulled his phone out. No word was spoken. No request made or suggestion given, but music filled the air in the next moment. When another moan came over the music, he just turned the volume up.

"Yep. The night's drama is finito."

Heather figured right.

We didn't all leave right away.

Mason sat, and I was tugged into his lap.

Channing and Heather mirrored us.

We talked with Nate and Matteo, and the group of four seemed content to do their own thing, and once in a while joining in with our conversation.

Logan and Taylor never joined us again.

10

SAMANTHA

We stayed up around the campfire until two in the morning.

We talked. We told stories. And we laughed, a lot.

At one point Zellman (the shorter one from Bren's crew) asked Matteo about his football prospects for next year, and a hush fell over the group.

"Z!" Bren hissed.

Jordan laughed.

Zellman didn't seem to give a care about what he asked.

Cross was eyeing the rest of us, a wariness coming over him, but it was the same wariness that I felt sometimes before I knew a fight might break out. Normal Sam and I'd feel the same sensation. Drunk Sam was distinctly disappointed because nothing popped off from that question.

Instead of replying, Matteo had looked at Mason. "I'm sorry for being an asshole again. Me not playing and you playing is not on you. That's my issue." A beat again. He was grimacing. "I have to say, I was jealous. I'm sorry."

Mason had leaned forward, resting his elbows on his knees and dipped his head to Matteo. "Appreciate that. Respect."

Matteo had then turned to Zellman. "And I'm not sure yet, but there *are* teams asking for me. I'll see what pans out."

Nate's grin turned sloppy and he raised the taped bottle, pretending to wipe the back of his hand over his forehead. "Thank God we didn't have to break out the sauna and hot coals for a session of Truth Time. That would've been embarrassing. I would've spilled about a kissing experience with a girl in seventh grade. The term *helicopter tongue* does not apply to French kissing." He burped, his cheeks all red. "And I have no idea why I decided to share that right now with you all..." His gaze lingered on Channing's sister and her friends, "...who are slightly less than strangers."

Zellman blinked, trying to focus, and leaned forward. "I'm glad you did." He sounded very serious. "Do you have a sister that has weird social skills?"

Bren and Cross shared a look.

Channing was suddenly frowning.

Nate frowned right along with him.

Matteo had then started hiccupping, which had his massive upper body twitching. It was almost violent, and it caused his chair to rattle each time as well. What was left in his bottle spilled out, and he was scrambling to save his booze at the same time he kept hiccupping. The rest of the group started laughing, and from then on, we were mostly laughing until we'd all headed to our beds.

The weird moment passed and no one brought it up again.

Heather had nudged me at one point, and I followed her gaze.

Bren and Cross were sneaking off from the group, and I had to marvel at how stealthy they were. Their two other friends had no clue. They were quiet, taking a couple steps back, and they blended in with the trees almost immediately. Skills. Serious skills there.

The next to go were Heather and Channing.

Mason and I left right after, but even when we went into our camper, we could hear the guys still talking for a long while. We fell asleep to their muted conversation, but now I was awake— awake to find my man was rising above me, then moving inside of me, and I was gone.

Pleasure slammed through me.

I wound my legs around Mason's hips, moving with him.

I rode him as he rode me, and he trailed kisses over my chin, his mouth finding mine, opening over mine.

"Fuck, Sam," he groaned into my ear, beginning to move a little faster. A little harder.

I was right there with him.

My body strained. I needed more. I always needed more.

This man, my shelter, my home—just mine. All mine.

Thousands loved him. His name was spoken on nationally televised networks, but he was mine.

And he was Maddie's father.

The three of us. We had created a family, and I hoped one day to have more children. I wound my arms around his shoulders, tightened my legs, and lifted my body to meet his until with a quiet growl (as quiet as those could be) he came inside of me.

I wasn't far behind, and once I'd finished, Mason raised himself up.

He didn't pull out or move off to the side. He moved his hand between us and worked me all over again until I exploded in his arms for a second time.

When I came down from my high, Mason was curled behind me, pressing the softest and most tender kisses over my back, my shoulders, my nape, down my spine, and back up.

I was half drowsing, feeling lazy, feeling satiated, and a hundred percent feeling happy. I ran my nail gently up and down the arm he had curved in front of me.

"Do you feel better about you and Matteo now?" I asked in a quiet voice.

He paused his kisses. "Yeah." His arms tightened around me. "I knew he'd get picked up. It's just a matter of time, but him saying that tonight helped."

"You think Logan and Taylor are okay?"

He paused, and I felt him tensing behind me. "Why are you asking?"

I peered at him. "I don't know. Just a feeling I got at moments today. I mean, Taylor didn't seem out of the ordinary, but I don't know. It's just there. I feel like something's going on with them."

"I don't know. He's been quiet a bit more lately, but I just figured that was law school. He said it's more intense than it was earlier in the year." Mason bent to my shoulder, kissing there.

I picked up his hand, lacing our fingers together. "I think it's the mama bear in me. I'm becoming Malinda. I want to make sure everyone is happy. You think everyone is happy?"

His lips moved over my skin as he spoke. "I think everything will work out. Nate's getting his shit sorted out. Matteo will get picked up by a team. Logan will share when he needs to. Or Taylor will say something to you too. If something is going on, they'll be fine. He needs her, and he knows that. Heather and Channing seem good. As for Channing's sister and her group, who the fuck knows with them. They kept talking about some Zeke guy and looking at me weird."

"Zeke?"

Instead of answering, Mason's hand moved between our bodies once more, and he found my spot, and I was a writhing mess before long—a sensual and very contented writhing mess. Then he moved over me once more.

We didn't get much sleep the rest of the night.

Mason asked if I wanted to try leapfrogging with him.

11

SAMANTHA

Logan had driven into the nearest town the next morning. He came back with the whole SUV loaded with donuts, fresh coffee, breakfast sandwiches, pancakes, and every egg order anyone could think up.

After everyone was full, we began to pack up to leave.

"So no big drama this trip," Heather said.

She moved to straddle the picnic bench where I was washing some of the dishes we'd used.

"Nope. No big drama."

She glanced at Logan and Taylor's camper. They'd been inside it for the last thirty minutes.

"Was it me or was Logan quieter than normal?"

I lowered the plate I was washing. "Yes, but Mason thinks it'll all be fine."

"They were lovey-dovey this morning."

They had been. Taylor sat in Logan's lap as they ate.

I nodded, piling the coffee mugs into a bin we'd take back with us. "Everyone seems like they had a good time. Did Bren and her crew?"

A ghost of a smile flashed on Heather's face. "You keep saying crew. You know that they actually are in a crew?"

I raised an eyebrow. "Say again?"

"You never say *group*. You've been saying *crew* this whole time."

"You said they're actually *in* a crew? What's that mean?"

"It was a system put in place in Roussou because of you."

Now both my eyebrows went up. "Say again?"

She laughed. "Yeah. 'Cause of you and Broudou."

"Brett?"

"No. Budd—with, you know, what he wanted to do. Channing rallied and got a crew together to go against Broudou."

I didn't know how to process that. I'd heard about the crew system, but it had never been fully explained to me.

Bren and her friends emerged from their camper then. Their arms were full of sleeping bags, blankets, and bags.

I set aside what dishes were left. "Did everything get worked out before? From you know…"

There'd been an arrest. Mason and Logan had gotten involved, or more specifically, their father had gotten involved.

Heather frowned. "Channing didn't tell you guys what really went down?"

I shook my head. "No, but I assumed everything was fine."

"Yeah. It worked out." A thoughtful look entered her eyes before she shook her head, clearing whatever she'd been thinking. "I *think* it's all good. I hope, anyways."

And that was the end of it because Mason and Channing were heading over.

They'd been packing up the vehicles, but as if they'd practiced it, they now rounded the table and dropped down next to their women.

"Hi." I smiled at Mason.

He reflected my look and leaned in. "Hi." Then his lips were on mine.

I heard Channing greeting Heather in the same way.

"What's the plan after this?" Nate asked as he slid onto the bench next to Mason.

He propped an elbow on the table, leaning forward to face the rest of us.

"Are you and Matteo interested in heading to Fallen Crest?" Mason asked. He nodded to Channing. "We're all going back to check in with family, and then we were going to head to Manny's tonight."

Nate seemed to mull that over before he bobbed his head up and down. "Yeah. I can do that. I wanna swing by the house anyways."

Mason and I shared a look.

A year ago, Nate would've meant our house. Even six months ago, he would've meant our place. But now, we both knew he meant his family's house.

Things had definitely changed.

Mason seemed to want to say something, but after a pause, he turned to Channing. "That's the plan?"

Channing had his arm around Heather's shoulders as she rested against his chest. He lowered his head slowly. "I'll round up the kids, and we'll take off. Six tonight?" He squeezed Heather's shoulder as he directed the question to her.

"Sounds good." She nodded. "Brandon will be happy to see you guys."

Nate's eyes lit up. "Brandon and Gus."

Heather groaned, "Don't talk about Gus. He's probably already drunk on the barstool as we're talking. And that's if Brandon sent him home after closing."

But Nate laughed. "I like Gus."

Heather retorted, "You're the only one then."

Nate didn't care. He just laughed harder.

After that, we disbanded to finish whatever was needed. Nate put the call in for the company to come back and get the campers. We loaded the vehicles, and an hour later, we all left caravan-style.

The drive back was relatively quiet.

Taylor and Logan were in the back.

We were an hour from Fallen Crest when it happened.

"Mom and Dad fucked us up," Logan said from the back.

The air shifted.

I felt everything dropping, becoming more grounded.

Mason looked in the rearview mirror toward his brother, but when I turned to look too, Logan was gazing out the window. Taylor watched him, and he gripped her hand as if it were his lifesaver. But his voice—I'd never get the sound of it out of my head, raw and guttural.

I'd never heard Logan speak like that.

"I've not thought about kids—having them or dealing with them," he continued. "Maddie's different. I loved her before she was born, and I know, I know that the same will happen for my own kids someday." He looked at Mason now, who briefly met his brother's gaze in the rearview mirror. "Dad was an absent, cheating asshole. Mom was an absent, alcoholic bitch. How the fuck are you going to be a dad?"

Mason was quiet, his eyes intense. He flexed his hands over the steering wheel before he replied, his voice gravelly. "I'll be the best fucking dad I never had. That's what I'll do, and FYI—there's a year between us, but I took care of *you*."

Logan nodded. "That's my point. I didn't. Growing up how we did, whatever—we took care of whoever was trying to hurt us. We looked out for the people we loved, but in college and now law school, I've not been thinking about that way of living. I've just been focused on school, whether I want to work for the company or look for a different law firm, how I can try to make junior partner as fast as I can. Spend as much time with you guys, with Maddie, with Nate and Matteo. That's been my life."

Mason glanced at me.

Where was this coming from? I looked at Taylor, but she seemed confused.

He swung his gaze to Taylor, his eyes haunted. "I don't know why it's hitting me today, but I need you, Taylor. Not that I didn't know before, but this is different. I don't know. Things just feel different right now. Jesus. I need you. Mase used to reel me in, but he's got a family now. I'm on my own. Nate doesn't do it. He doesn't know how to do it, and that's your job. You've taken it up, always knowing me more than I know myself, loving me more than I deserve. I'm an asshole."

A sheen of tears glistened in Taylor's eyes, but she didn't let them fall. "Stop, Logan," she whispered. "I've been worried. I knew something was going on with you, but I didn't push. Or I was going to push later when we were alone, but Logan. You love me and you take care of me just fine."

Her voice dropped even lower, but we could still hear.

"You know I have things in me. What happened to my mom changed me inside, but you made me alive. You made me love. You helped me become me, and don't ever think about you or me. I ground you, but you make me come alive. That's how *we* are."

He leaned closer to her, dropping his voice.

They were both murmuring quieter and I sat forward, giving them privacy.

My phone buzzed just as I noticed Mason watching me.

He turned back to the road, but reached over and laced our fingers together.

Not much needed to be said.

We'd all been through hell and back.

We were in a different stage of our lives. Marriage. Children. Careers. Responsibilities got heavier, more serious. People depended on you. Lives depended on you. Logan's fears made sense to me. I'd had Analise growing up, and there'd been a lot of moments when I worried I'd be just like her. But I wasn't. Never.

There'd not been one moment where I felt myself slipping into what I had seen growing up.

I was not Analise. Mason already wasn't, and Logan would not be Helen or James.

Everything would be just fine.

Feeling my phone buzz again, I opened it up. It was a picture of my little girl.

I scrolled through, seeing two recent uploads. In one she had passed out in my dad's arms, a limp noodle, and in the other one she was crawling on the floor, with flour everywhere! Flour in her hair, her hands, on her legs, and she was so happy. I could hear her squeal when that picture was taken.

An overwhelming sense of peace rose up in me.

I squeezed Mason's hand and showed him the pictures. The way he laughed, so full of tenderness, almost beat out the way his eyes softened. Almost. Not quite.

He melted for his little girl, and I knew what Logan was worried about wouldn't happen.

We were not our parents.

We would be better.

12

SAMANTHA

I was staring at heaven.

Mason was shirtless, lying on the bed beside me and Maddie was curled in his arms. Her head was turned into his neck and he was cradling her and just watching her.

After we got to Fallen Crest, we headed to Malinda's and my dad's house. We were back in my old bedroom in the basement. I'd needed sleep. Any time you go camping, there's a necessary recuperation/hibernation time period afterwards and Mason, bless him, and had volunteered to stay up with Maddie when she got fussy.

Seeing I was awake, he said softly, "Hey. You feel more rested?"

I nodded, sitting up, and I reached for her. It was just automatic. That was my little girl.

He shifted, handing her, then bending down and kissing her forehead first and then mine. He eased out of bed not to wake her as she started nestling into me. "Bathroom. Be back." He trailed a hand down my arm as he left.

She'd need to be fed soon, but until then, I eased back against the headboard and held Maddie, breathing her smell in. Heaven. Pure heaven.

It wasn't long before Mason came back and eased right back in his place. He moved up to sit next to me, curling an arm around me so he was holding both of us, and he moved his head, kissing my temple. "Malinda's obsessed."

I grinned. He wasn't lying.

We came back and Malinda had a whole scene where she tried to get us to leave again. We didn't, but she was firm. "Now, you go. Shoo. I need more grandma time." When she got that we weren't actually leaving, she caved, but we got grumbles and glowers for the next couple hours before I went down for a nap.

I said now, "Maddie was in a good mood when we got back. Mama Malinda needs to be called Grandma Malinda now, and if we ever moved back, she'd be our nanny."

His arm tightened around me. "Maybe we should do that."

I looked up, frowning. "What?"

His eyes were on Maddie. "During off-season. We could get a house here, come back and stay. You can train wherever. And I know you love running up in the hills. Then when we need to go back for football, we go back."

I smoothed a hand down Maddie's little back. "You'd be okay with that?"

He shrugged. "Yeah. Why not? I mean, there are reasons you want to be closer to Heather too."

Yeah.

"We can afford two houses?"

He nodded. "Oh yeah. I mean, I have a good salary with the team, but Logan and I both have money from our dad's company too. We've not really touched that money, or I haven't. I don't think Logan has either."

I'd forgotten about that money.

"It'll be fine. We don't need to worry about that stuff, and if we did, we could downsize at one of the houses. Real estate is usually a good investment too."

Maddie moved, and we both held our breaths. Waiting.

Then she settled back in, just moving her head, finding me, and her entire body relaxed.

Mason smiled faintly. "She knows she's in her mom's arms."

I smiled back.

Man. I loved my family.

Running another hand down Maddie's back, it wasn't just her. It wasn't just Mason. It was all of them. Logan. Taylor. Heather. All our friends. But my dad. Malinda. Even Analise was better. James was still an asshole, but he was mostly fine to me. He kept the asshole parts to deal with Mason and Logan, and Mason usually never let me hear about those calls. But I knew they happened.

James wanted both boys at his company. Both boys didn't want that. There were arguments.

But also Garrett, my biological father, and Sheila.

Yes. I was blessed, very blessed.

Mason spoke up, "I think Logan and Taylor are heading to Cain tomorrow to see her dad."

"So we have tonight."

"We have tonight."

I glanced around, but didn't see the clock. "What time is it?"

Mason stiffened, but said, "Almost time to go. Heather texted your phone thirty minutes ago. I told her we'd be late, that I didn't want to wake you."

"You did?"

He shot me a look. "You need sleep, Sam. Heather understood. Everyone understood."

"Oh." I relaxed again.

"But Malinda is chomping at the bit. She wants grandma babysitting duty while we get ready and go. Heather mentioned

there's a Roussou thing going on, so Channing's friends will be at
Manny's too."

I shook my head as Mason got out of bed, then went to the
door. "It still makes me laugh that when Roussou has things
going on, they come to a bar in Fallen Crest."

Mason gave me a grin before he opened the door.

Malinda was there. "Ooooh! There's my girl."

Both of us hushed her, and immediately Malinda's voice went
from a six to a one and she was cooing all over Maddie. She came
over, slid her arms under my little girl, and stood back, cradling
her to her shoulder. She skimmed over me. "You're looking more
rested. Your color's a bit better."

She leaned over, adjusting Maddie, and ran a hand through
my hair.

"Oh yes. You need another night with friends." She straightened back up, moving to the door. "Off you both go. Shower. Get
ready. I'm going to call Roy to come and drive you guys—"

"No." Mason stopped her. "I'll drive."

"Roy's like our own taxi driver. He's local and young.
He'll be—"

"No. I'm not going to drink more than one beer. I'm good to
drive us home."

She raised an eyebrow. "You sure?"

He dipped his head. "I'm sure, but I appreciate the thought."
He nodded to Maddie. "You helping out so fast is more than
enough of a thank-you. We know we won't always have a
babysitter at hand."

Malinda stared at him, long and hard. Then she started blinking, and she kept blinking. She looked at me and sniffled. "You're
my kids. Neither came from my loins, but you're my kids. Means
the world to me. You know that. And this little girl, she's the first
and I'll always want to babysit. As long as I can get around in a
wheelchair, I get grandma duty. You got that?" Her voice rose and
she gave us both sharp looks.

"Got that?"

We hadn't answered quick enough.

"Got it." Mason smiled, gentling his tone.

She gave me a pointed look. "You gotta say it, Sam. I get grandma duty first because I know the rest are already starting to wake up, getting their heads out of the asses, but I'm already here. I've been here since the first day I met you all."

She had, and I had no problem telling her she got grandma duty first.

She heard my words, and she kept blinking, then a tear slipped free and she said gruffly, "You both get ready to go. I've got a grandchild to love on."

Mason shut the door behind her. His eyes darkened, taking me in. "You need to pump?"

I did. I was hurting. I'd pumped yesterday and this morning, but I needed to do it again. Pump and dump.

He left, coming back with everything I needed. After that, he showered and got ready. When I was done, I bypassed him for the shower. When I came back, he'd taken care of everything. The bed was made. My purse was sitting on top. My phone next to it, and even my sandals were on the floor right next to the bed.

He'd thought of everything.

Grabbing my things, I headed upstairs and Mason was playing with Maddie. Her happy shrieks filled the entire house.

Malinda and my dad were standing in the kitchen. I moved to both, giving each a hug and a kiss on the cheek, then I had a whole moment with Maddie. Moms needed these sometimes. I needed mine, and no one said a word. I had to do a hug, a kiss, then another hug. Then I needed to nuzzle into her neck, getting my own gleeful shriek from her, and then I was okay until later tonight.

Mason waited at the door.

I handed Maddie off, another soft kiss to her forehead, and he held his hand out.

I took it. He led me outside.

He held my hand the entire drive to Manny's.

13

SAMANTHA

Manny's was full, and when I say full, I meant cars and trucks were parked on the street. There was a line getting into the door, and I'd never seen Manny's this packed. They'd been spreading out at a constant pace over the last couple years. Opening the back end. Renovating the back end. Adding on to the back end. Revamping the section behind Manny's. Then revamping and adding on to the right side of Manny's, not to mention at some point they'd totally redone the outside front section too. I knew that'd been done a ways back, but I had no clue when.

"Wow."

Mason frowned, pulling up to the front entrance.

I glanced at the side door. It was still there, but the chairs Heather and I used to sit at for our breaks were no longer there. I missed our 'smoke' breaks, meaning that Heather smoked and I sat, and we both took our breaks together.

The bones of the old Manny's were still there, but everything else looked shiny and new.

I'd never admit this to Heather because business was

booming for her, and that meant good things like franchising, but I missed the old Manny's. I missed when only the regulars like Gus knew about it, but this was very, very good for Heather. Hence, me not even uttering those words to anyone except in my own head.

"I'll drop you off, then park somewhere."

"You sure?"

Mason nodded, scanning Manny's behind me. "Logan said they're in a corner table inside. I can see why we aren't outside."

Yeah. The outside looked overrun by high school students. Or college students.

I reserved the right to now put them all in the same category, because they all looked young to me. Even though we were only out of college not far ourselves.

Heading in, I used the side door (sentimental reasons), but a giant guy was suddenly there and in my space. He was giant and bald, and he was holding a beer. He was also looking at me like I was dirt under his shoe. "This door's closed. You gotta go to the front if you're coming in."

One, the door wasn't closed. I walked through it just fine.

And two, I was just pissed. I had no number two.

I opened my mouth, but suddenly Brandon was hurrying down from behind the bar. "Moose, she's good. That's family."

Moose didn't seem convinced. I wasn't under his shoe anymore, but he was doing a good impression of a mean girl. I was just under his nose this time. "Your name?"

Brandon cleared his throat, now coming from behind the bar. "This is Samantha Kade." And he was catching me up, giving me a hug. "It's good to see you, Sam. Heather said Drunk Sam made an appearance last night, and I know those appearances can hold her over for a year."

I laughed, but hugged Heather's brother back. "It's good to see you."

Brandon let me go, his eyes trailing over my shoulder. "This is Heather's best friend. Chill or Heather will rip your balls off."

I looked and the giant goliath now was looking more like a teddy bear. His cheeks were a little pink. "I'm real sorry. I should know who you are."

I didn't get that, but I just shrugged. "You're one of Channing's, right?"

He gave me a brief nod. "You're correct."

Brandon's hand came to my arm, just as he started to return behind the bar. "Heather's in the office. We had some staff issues, but you can head on over. They're at the table on the other side of the bar."

We had prime seating. There was another door, one that wasn't being barred, to one side of our table. The restrooms were just down the hallway. The bar was within four feet of us, and the kitchen staff were coming and going from the counter on the other side. Oh yes. Heather put us here on purpose. I knew my girl, and this way she could keep an eye on everything in Manny's and still see us.

I loved my girl. Brilliant.

I was just heading to the table when said girl was coming out of her office, looking aggrieved. Her eyes lit on me and she nodded, her face brightening. She passed the table, heading my way, and we hugged as our greeting.

"This is insane, right?" She pulled back, glancing around.

"Kinda, but good for you. Right?"

Her eyebrows went up. There were bags under her eyes. She started to massage at her temples. "Roussou is having a festival this weekend. A bunch of alumni from the high school are in town, so somehow that translated into coming over here."

"Where's Channing?" I scanned the table. He wasn't there.

"He's at his bar. They're overrun with college kids."

I frowned. "Wasn't that a biker bar?"

"It was, until the college kids moved in. It is a biker bar during the week, but during the weekend, they started coming over here." She gestured in the back. "You don't see 'em, but there's a bunch of bikers in the back back. Not the back room, but the back section between here and the house. I had them move all their bikes to the other side of the house too." A worried look flashed, and she hesitated a second. "I need to warn you that I heard rumors Shannon Broudou was in town."

Whoa.

Blast from the past, and not a welcomed one.

"What's she doing nowadays?"

Heather shrugged. "Not a clue. I heard once she was dead, then I heard she was divorced. Next I heard she was in a trailer park somewhere. I wouldn't be surprised if she came here on the back of a bike."

I frowned. "I thought there were issues with a local MC?"

Another shrug as Heather returned to scanning the place. "There was, but I don't want to get into it. It's complicated now, but they stop for a beer here and at Channing's place." She nodded in the direction of where I'd first come in. "Chan sent some of his guys here for crowd control and if anything starts up."

So, same old Manny's because things tended to 'start up' here. And frequently.

I relaxed a little hearing that. It felt more familiar.

"Where's Mason?"

"He dropped me off and went to park."

"Shit. I should've texted you guys. I kept a couple spots open by the house."

I was about to suggest I could text him when I turned, and he was coming in. Unlike me, Moose didn't stop him. He saw Mason, dipped his head, and held up his beer in salute. Mason reached over, his fist meeting Moose's fist around his drink, and they exchanged a few words. Moose pointed at me, and Mason turned.

Seeing me, his eyes hitting mine, he said something more to Moose before starting his way toward me.

That's when the buzz started.

Buzz that it took a second to penetrate because I was lost, just watching Mason. Yep. I was still feeling the hormones from a happy baby, happy family, and feeling how he'd taken care of me today and a whole bunch during the night.

Then the looks started.

The whispers.

Mason ignored it all, coming over to me, and nodding to Heather at the same time he tugged me in front of him. My back was to his front, and he linked one arm around my chest, anchoring me to him. "How goes it, Heather? Place is looking good."

Heather wasn't listening to him.

She tuned into the reaction Mason was getting and cursed under her breath. "Forgot about this. I shouldn't have. I remembered it when we picked our campsite, but you're you and I've known you for years now. And you don't act anything except normal, but yeah. You're in your hometown, and if you haven't clued in, Mason, you're a bit of a star here."

Mason grimaced, tightening his arm around me. "Let's just ignore them?"

Heather laughed. "That's not going to do a damned thing." Her eyes trailed past us and she nodded. "See. My point. I'm going to have to figure something out because this could get bad."

"Mr. Kade?"

It was a little kid.

Which startled me because Manny's was a bar, but I forgot that during day hours, it was a restaurant pub for families too. We were getting to the cutoff time when families needed to head home, but until then, a little dude who looked ten years old was looking at Mason like he could leap mountains and move rivers.

"Can I have your autograph?" He held up a pen and paper,

then leaned in and whispered loudly, "It's for me, but it's really for my dad. He's too embarrassed to come over, but I'm not supposed to tell you that. So I didn't actually tell you that. K?" And he blinked, smiling so wide that I melted all over again.

I wanted a little boy now.

I had my girl, but I wanted a boy.

Mason knelt down and did his thing.

He was always good with the kids and the teenagers. Every now and then, we'd get a teen with an attitude, and when that happened, the old Mason came out. He was able to 'check' the teen quick. Only a few times did they get pissed, but people got weird when they're close to fame. I hadn't a clue why, but I noticed it enough to know it happened.

It was the women he had no time for, and sometimes the older guys got a bit much too. If a guy wanted to have a beer with Mason or wanted to sit and become his best friend. The women wanted to sleep with him, and if I was with him, I got eyed up as to who I was and how they could get me gone. Those were the moments I knew the old Mason was still there, because when I said that Mason could be a dick, he really could be a dick.

Tonight, I wasn't sure what we were going to end up with, especially considering Logan was with us too.

A line had started, but Mason gestured for me to go sit down.

I did, but only because he moved over so he was standing right next to me. I kept a hand on his back, a touch that I knew he appreciated, and the rest of us tried to pretend everything was normal.

We were all here sans Channing.

Heather popped in when she could and stayed as long as she could. Her mouth got tighter and tighter when the line for Mason's autograph wasn't getting shorter. And that happened sometimes too. There'd be an initial wave, but then people would return to their normal tables. When that happened, Mason could be normal again.

That wasn't happening this time, and it wasn't just bothering Heather.

Logan's eyes were getting more and more narrow as the time went on.

Nate was drinking his beer, but he'd stopped twenty minutes ago. His looks from Logan, to Heather, to me, to Mason were getting more frequent, though.

Taylor started doing the same as Nate, but she was mostly focused on Logan and how Logan was getting more and more tense. Matteo got his fair share of autographs too, at first. His line had stopped an hour ago.

Then finally, Heather came over and stopped right next to Mason. "Okay." She moved in, plucking a pen from a kid and pushing it back at his chest. "Zeke, get gone."

"What?" The kid wasn't really a kid. He looked like a future frat brother, blond hair and broad shoulders. "He's my hero, Heather."

Heather and Zeke were on a first-name basis? Interesting.

"No. Out. Now."

"But—"

"Zeke."

And that was totally unexpected, because that came from Nate and everyone's head swung around. He was giving Zeke a hard look, his eyebrows pinched together. "I'll get you an autograph later. Mason wants to sit with friends. Give him that respect, yeah?"

Zeke scowled at him, but then shrugged. "Fine."

He took the pen from Heather and said, "You used to be my favorite of the women." He leaned in, hissing, "No longer, Ms. Jax. No. Longer." He lifted his head, his gaze going to the other side of Logan. "I can't fan on Mrs. Kade, so I'm all about the Mrs. Logan now. Your loss, Jax."

Heather rolled her eyes, but her mouth was fighting from

grinning. "I'll take my loss and bear it, Zeke. Get gone. Restaurant is closing. Get all your friends out of here with you."

He grunted, but turned and let out a shrill whistle.

A large portion of people quieted, looking over.

He raised a hand up. "FCA, head out. Party's at my place."

And, just as surprisingly, everyone started leaving.

He glanced back. "When you're at an extended family holiday, and Cross is bitching about me, you remember this moment, Jax. You stick up for me."

Heather was having none of it. "Get gone or I'm siccing Moose on you."

That hurried him up, and he headed out, but not before saluting Heather with two fingers in the air.

Heather's mouth was pressed tight, and as soon as he was gone, she snorted, shaking her head. "That kid. Seriously." She looked at Mason. "He's obsessed with you, so I'm telling you now to watch out for your future stalker. He's a punk, but I swear, sometimes you almost like the damned kid." She seemed to be talking to herself, but then sighed. "Right. I'll get you guys more beer."

And she did just that.

Or, Brandon did that, because once all the high schoolers cleared out and the families who'd come in for a Saturday night meal, there was a lot more room. He brought over three pitchers, asking over the table at the same time, "Moose said Channing could use them. You want to keep them or let them loose?"

Heather's eyes narrowed. "Reds still out back?"

"Some."

Mason questioned, "Reds?"

"Red Demons. A couple chapters came to town for Roussou's festival."

"Thought that stuff was over?"

I repeated Heather's earlier words, "It's complicated."

Heather shot me a grin, but then there was a shout from

across the bar. A shorter version of the giant who'd blocked me had his arms spread wide. "Yo. People are coming in. Should we let 'em in or not?"

Heather groaned, glanced to her brother a second before waving. "Yeah. Let 'em in."

And with that said, the night activities had officially commenced.

14

BREN

"Place is closed. What are we doing out here?" Zellman asked, standing on the back of Jordan's truck, his hand held out toward Manny's. "We're not of age. Jax ain't going to let us in."

Cross was frowning at me, but I knew he wouldn't speak up.

Jordan was frowning at me too, but mostly looking confused.

There was a tone with Zellman.

I asked, "You pissed or something?"

"Yeah! I want to go see my girl. There are parties going on. Let's go *there*, not *here*."

"What's going on, Bren?"

I swung my gaze to Jordan. Both he and Cross were standing outside the truck. Cross was leaning with one shoulder our way, but Jordan had both his shoulders facing us. His hands were clasped together, his elbows resting over the back of the truck's bed.

I shrugged. "I don't know. It's just a feeling. We can't leave, not yet."

"Fucking Zeke is throwing a party. He invited everyone there.

We could go there. We're missing that shit, 'cause you got a feeling?"

Both Cross and Jordan shot Zellman with a glare.

"Fucking chill, Z. She's saved your ass plenty of times 'cause of one of those 'feelings.'"

Cross' phone started ringing. He pulled it out, showing us the screen.

Taz calling.

Jordan snickered. "You know your sister's at Zeke's wondering why we ain't there."

Cross groaned, but answered and moved away a little. "Hey."

His head folded and he paused, listening.

A beat later, "Yeah, yeah. We know. We're waiting for something, then we'll head there. You're not alone, right?"

Taz started talking. All of us could hear Cross' twin's voice, but we couldn't make out her words. Thirty seconds later, Cross was saying goodbye and coming back. He put his phone back in his pocket, saying to us, "She said there are no parties in Roussou. Everyone is headed to Zeke's."

Jordan made a face, his eyes widening. "Thought we hated that fucker?"

Zellman snorted. "We do. We did, but we don't hate his parties. Best free booze around, man."

Cross went back to watching me, and I went back to remaining silent. A feeling. Just a feeling.

I knew who was in there. I knew they probably didn't need help. They could handle their own, had handled their own when they were our age, but a feeling. I couldn't get around the feeling.

If we left, bad.

If we went inside, bad too.

So, staying. Not bad.

That's what I was feeling and it was infuriating, but it was there.

It was another hour later when I found out why I had that feeling.

15

SAMANTHA

Once the restaurant had closed and the entire place became the bar, it was just as busy.

The grill remained open for appetizers, but an hour later that closed. Then, the drinks flowed. And flowed, they did indeed.

Shots were called out every minute.

People had a drinking table in the corner. That was new. People could head over and lie down for body shots. There was a mural in a corner of two giant angel wings and people could stand in the middle and take photos. That was a hit.

More than a few guys came over, trying to buy Mason a shot.

He turned them down, and after twenty minutes, I could tell he was getting pissed. People were pushing the drinks and Mason didn't like getting drunk. He was saying no, and for Mason, he was being polite.

Then he snapped.

A guy was waving a shot in the air. "Come on, man. One shot."

"I said no, dude."

"Come on!"

That, by itself wasn't too annoying. But that, said for the tenth time in a row, and Mason slapped the shot out of his hand he shoved upright. "I fucking said no," he growled, towering over the guy.

Chairs scraped back.

Logan was at Mason's side immediately.

Matteo and Nate moved at the same time, shoving the drunk guy back. His arm was twisted around his back, and he was marched to the door. He got booted out. The whole thing happened in a couple seconds, so the guy was to the door before he realized what happened. He started hollering then. "Hey! What the fuck? That asshole thinks he's hot and mighty? You ain't nothing, bruh. Nothing. You're slime and your woman—"

Mason growled, starting for him.

Logan jerked in front, slapping a hand to Mason's chest, but he didn't stop. He did a circle, saying to Mason, "Stay." And he completed his circle, moving for the guy.

Matteo was focused on the guy, so he didn't see Logan coming.

Nate did, and his eyes got big, but then he braced, holding the guy captive. He was setting him up and then Logan was right there. The guy didn't see that either.

"What'd you say, motherfucker?" Logan taunted once before he barked, "Let him go!"

Nate did, dropping his hands and stepping back.

Matteo was still focused on containing the struggling guy, but when the guy swung free from Nate's side, he swung into Matteo and he used his fist to do it.

"What the hell?" That was Matteo as he took a hit to his head. He let him go, but before he could round on him, the guy was gone. He launched himself at Logan, who was waiting, who was salivating.

The guy went at Logan.

Logan ducked, then grabbed the back of the guy's head. He pulled him down and brought his knee up.

The guy paused, shaking his head.

The guy had friends.

"Fucking rich assholes," one guy growled, coming in from the restaurant tables, and he was wearing a leather cut.

Heather saw and swore. She raked a hand down her face. "This ain't good." She cast a look at me, but Mason was already moving me.

He sent me to Heather. "Put her in the office."

Heather reached out, taking my arm, but she didn't move. Neither did I.

We could only watch, stunned and horrified as more guys joined in the fight. That was, until someone was coming from the back, saw the fight, paused, and yelled back, "Demons! Fight!" There was a stampede of guys after that, all rushing from the back section, streaming past us and wading in.

One guy caught Mason from behind and I saw red. "Hell no!"

Heather's hand clamped tighter on mine. "Sam. No."

Nope. No. They weren't going to hurt my man. I didn't care if they were big and scary and I was an eighth of their weight. Oh hell no.

I started forward, but Heather yanked me back. "Taylor?"

Logan's girlfriend grabbed me and both of them started pulling me backwards, but Heather stopped. "What—shit!" She let go, tearing across the bar, weaving through the fight, which now included Brandon, an older guy that I was pretty certain was Gus, Matteo, Mason, Logan, Nate, and the two guys I knew were Channing's friends against who I was assuming were the Red Demons.

There were a lot more Red Demons and those motorcycle guys knew how to fight.

I didn't want to find out who won. I knew our guys would do more damage than was expected.

A lot more damage.

Then, a flare shot up in the bar, half blinding everyone. Some of the guys took cover, but the others paused in their fighting and all looked to where the flare came from.

Holding it, standing in the side doorway, was Bren.

She raked everyone with a look of death. "You all know who I am."

Two things happened then.

Heather cursed, yelling for her staff to cover whatever might start burning. And two, one of the older Red Demons broke free. He'd been holding back Matteo and he started for her. "Bren, honey—"

She turned that death look on him. She was cold, *ice* cold. "Don't you dare 'honey' me." She still held the flare gun and motioned to Heather who was now ignoring the confrontation. She was trying to keep her place from catching on fire. "You all care about my brother and Heather. I don't know what started this fight, but I'm telling you that both of them care about these people." She indicated the guys and where Taylor and I stood.

"Bren. Sweetheart." From the older guy again.

He took another step forward.

She jerked back. "I know who you are. I know what you can do, what you can order, but I'm telling you to step back. Ask what started the fight, and then figure a way where you don't hurt every person that my brother cares about."

The older guy stood there. He studied her and rubbed a hand over his jaw. "We got the call that one of our brothers was in trouble. We see fighting, we wade in."

"Channing considers them family. One is like his best friend."

"Babe."

"I'm not babe. Don't do that to me. You know my story." She gentled her tone. "Don't do that to me."

He stared at her again.

The whole room was tense, waiting.

She added, "You fight them. You fight me."

The ripple of danger was still there, and at her words, it seemed to triple. It was still probing, and I swore, all of us were holding our breaths.

I mean, I knew they weren't, but pins and needles. Pins and needles.

Then the guy's head lowered and he turned to the group. "Who started the fight?"

One of the Red Demons stepped forward, but Mason spoke first. "One of your guys was pushing a drink on me. I can handle a few, but when I say no to the tenth one and I do it politely, I get pissed when I'm then turned on and insulted."

The older guy stared at Mason, his head cocked to the side. "You're that football guy?"

Mason nodded. "Yeah."

He looked at Bren. "The best friend?"

She nodded, her neck tight. "He's close to Channing, yes." She found me then, and I felt zapped.

Those eyes of her. The pain she was letting me see.

I knew, without a doubt, that no one else was seeing what I saw. She had it covered up. They were getting the wall she was showing, and that was a fierce wall in here. It was jarring, but I saw behind it. I saw the emptiness there.

I felt the agony. I felt it as if it were my own. The pain sliced me, and for a second, I was rendered speechless.

It didn't matter.

She was talking, "That one had a baby not long ago. They're in town. They camped with us last night, and they're having a beer with Heather because I'm assuming they're all heading off to their lives tomorrow."

Something registered with the older guy, and he looked back to Mason. "You're James Kade's boy?"

Logan sidled next to Mason, his eyes cold and narrowed. "We both are."

The older guy nodded slowly. His eyebrows were furrowed and his mouth tightened. But then he swung around and barked, "Calder. Who started the fight?"

The original other Red Demon that started forward before Mason spoke first, then nodded. "Hyena was pushing drinks on the guy. He was out of place, and when he got escorted out, he swung on that one." He indicated Matteo before looking at Logan. "Before he rushed *that* one. All hell broke loose after that."

The older guy drew in a breath. "Fight's on us then."

Calder dipped his head. "Yes."

"Well. Shit."

Calder agreed, "Well, shit indeed."

The older guy looked at Bren. "Good thing you got a flare gun on you, Little Monroe." His tone was teasing.

Bren rolled her eyes, handing the flare gun to one of her guys. All three were there, and I just noticed them. They had positioned themselves around her. The golden guy was slightly in front. The tall one to her side. The shorter one on her other side, but behind her too. They were having her back, literally.

The older took note too, nodding to them. "Heard word about you four. Heard word that you all got respect in your school."

It seemed an odd thing to say to high schoolers, and this guy was in his older forties? Fifties? He looked young, but he obviously wasn't. There was an aged depth to him at the same time, but I was also feeling other things about him too. He was smart, dangerous, and ruthless.

Not a clue why I was feeling that, but I was, and my gut was telling me that all my loved ones needed to be far away from this guy. Far, far away. As if sensing my uneasiness, Taylor's hand slid into mine and she squeezed. She sent me a half-grin.

I sent one back, returning her hand squeeze.

Bren didn't respond.

The golden one did, and his eyes matched Bren's empty ones. "No offense, Mr. Maxwell, but Monroe speaks for us."

I was going out on a limb and guessing that he wasn't meaning the Monroe standing with him.

That seemed to be the exact thing to say because the older guy suddenly started laughing. He shook his head, his hand raking over his face before he shook his hand toward them, but in a good-natured way. "I got your message, kid. Loud and clear. You're a smart one." He turned to Calder, grinning. "Give enough cash to Monroe's woman, buy that table a round, and let's head out. Boys need to fight, so let's go find a justified one." He turned to Heather. "Apologies, Mrs. Channing."

Heather huffed out, rolling her eyes. "You know we ain't married, Maxwell."

His mouth twitched. "All the same." Then he made a motion. "Let's go. Everyone out."

It was a similar call to action as the other high school, but the two seemed a world apart.

I had to shake my head at the surrealness of everything, because like that Zeke kid, these grown and dangerous leather-wearing-cut motorcycle club members all heeded their leader's call. One by one, they left until Calder was the last one left. He went to Heather, handing over a wad of cash. He said something to her, then placed the cash on a table and headed behind his group.

A roar of motorcycles sounded a little later, coming from the back of Manny's.

"Are you kidding me? A flare, Bren?"

Heather didn't waste time, now that Manny's was safe from not burning down. She was lighting into Channing's sister.

She didn't get a chance to do more.

The three guys closed in, forming an actual wall, and Heather had to stop short. "Move."

The tall and shorter ones didn't say a word. They also didn't move.

The golden one spoke, "Step back, Heather."

"You don't talk back to me, Cross. Not here. Not in my business."

He was keeping an even tone. "I'm not meaning to disrespect you, but I'm also not going to let you lay into Bren. She had a feeling we couldn't leave, so we didn't. Her feeling was right, and now, we *will* leave."

I looked behind them, but Bren was gone. The door was swinging shut, and before Heather could say anything more, the shorter one went next, the taller one, and the golden one remained. He held Heather's gaze. "She had a feeling, Heather. That's it."

Heather mashed her lips together, not looking appeased. Not by a long shot.

"Cross, I swear—" She sighed, closing her eyes. "Make sure she's okay."

"Always."

He said his piece and he was gone the next instant.

Heather stared at the door for another moment before she looked our way. "I need a drink." She raised her voice, "Manny's is closed. Everyone out except if I camped with you last night." Then, "And my brother."

Brandon just laughed. "Like fuck I'd leave anyways."

"What about me?"

Heather sighed. "Fine. You too, Gus."

16

BREN

"You okay?"

I was glad Cross waited this long to ask me. It was after leaving Manny's, once we all hopped into Jordan's truck and no one said a word. Jordan drove to my house where Cross and I hopped out. He and Z went to the party, which was the norm for us. If they needed us, they'd call. Until then, I still wasn't a party person, though I'd been trying more lately.

I nodded as we walked up to Channing's house.

I guess it was my house too, but it still felt like his. It'd always feel like his house. My home was over a few blocks with a ghost inside.

And as the usual for us, Cross didn't push. He and I walked inside.

He and I went to the kitchen.

He and I did our own thing.

He made a snack for himself, usually a sandwich.

I grabbed some water.

When we were done, he and I went to my room.

We got ready for bed, then climbed in and I turned for him as he turned for me.

He and I.

Tonight, though, tonight was different. It felt different, but I couldn't explain it.

He propped himself up on an elbow, looking down at me. "You gotta talk, Bren."

I looked back at him. "Like you do?"

I scored a point.

He flicked his eyes upwards, but settled back down next to me. He grabbed my hand, drawing both our hands up to his chest where he began to fiddle and play with my fingers. "You talked to the Red Demons tonight. That's pretty huge for you."

Yeah...

I didn't want to go there. He knew what they meant for me.

He tugged on my hand, turning his head to see me. "What do you think they were even doing here? Or doing at Manny's?"

I shook my head, rolling it slightly over my pillow. "I don't know." Channing would know. And if he didn't, Channing would deal with it. That's what he did. He handled any threats against Roussou, or against his loved ones.

"Your brother will be pissed about what happened tonight."

"I know." I sighed.

"He'll be out for a while, right?"

I grinned at him. "Yeah."

His eyes went past me to where I'd put my phone. "You should call him, get that over with. You know he'll want to check in with you at some point tonight."

It was Channing's way.

Cross was right, so I reached over and dialed my brother, putting him on speaker. It was always more fun this way.

Bar noises were almost deafening when he answered, "Tell me you're home and you're in bed, and you're *alone*."

Cross flashed a grin.

I refrained from laughing. "I'm in bed and I'm home."

Silence.

I knew he was at his bar. It would've been insane over there this weekend too.

He cursed into the phone. "I know we do this song and dance, but seriously, Bren. Please don't get pregnant."

Cross started laughing.

Channing growled, "I will fuck you up, little Shaw. You know I can and you know I will."

Cross stopped laughing, but took my phone and raised it closer to his mouth. "Bren's not going to get pregnant. You were the one—"

"Yeah, yeah. You two say the same shit. You know that, right?" He pretended to mimic us, raising his voice "'For all the shit we do, you did it ten times worse at our age.'" He dropped his voice back, more rough. "Yeah, well, you little fucks, I love you, but I do *not* want to be a grandfather so soon. You can't have a kid before I have a kid. Got it, Bren? Cross?"

I was fighting another smile at his grandfather term, but said, "Got it, Chan."

Cross was quiet.

"Shaw," my brother snapped.

Cross smirked at me, saying into the phone, "Do you feel some semblance of control by saying the same shit to us? Then us saying the same shit to you?"

"It makes me not want to come home and beat the shit out of you," Channing snapped from his end. "That's what it does for me. It'll help me get through one more night, and your ass had better be downstairs sleeping, *alone*, when I get home."

Cross went back to laughing. "Yes, sir."

Another savage growl bit out. "Love you guys."

I grinned faintly at the phone, saying it back, "Love you too."

Cross didn't respond, but that was okay.

Channing did love us. Cross loved him too. It was a different dynamic, and maybe because of that call, Cross and I just kissed a little. We cuddled. There was some making out, but we fell asleep respecting Channing's wishes.

Though, my brother would never be told this.

17

MASON

S am was sleeping. Maddie was sleeping.

I snuck out and headed to the old house.

Once I pulled in, Logan left and he climbed in, yawning. "Fucking early, bro. What are we doing here?"

I reversed as I answered, "That guy asked who we were to our dad. I talked to Channing last night. That guy's a big deal with a motorcycle club. He was not happy when he heard what happened."

Logan yawned again, leaning forward a bit. "Guessing Heather or his sister weren't real forthcoming with the details?"

I smirked. What Heather and the sister said was none of our business.

"So we're what again? Again. Fucking early, Mase. Too fucking early to be leaving my woman in a nice and warm bed, where I could slide in somewhere else that nice and warm, you get me?"

I grunted, "I get you, but I want to deal with this before shit hits the fan. It might not be anything. It might be something. Dad's at the country club, meeting some bigwig for an early morning tee time."

Logan groaned, his head falling back to the headrest, "Shit. That means we're going to be walking."

I threw him a sideways look. "We're going to be standing off against our dad. You're groaning about walking?"

"One." He flung his hand up. "I do not groan about anything except during sexual activities. Two, yes, I'm complaining about walking because anytime you give me a text saying, 'Get your ass up. Gotta meet,' I know shit is going to go down. That means I have to be alert up here." He tapped his head. "But the body, the body is still back there about to come down on Taylor. You feel me?"

"Whatever."

Then spying a coffee place, I swung in. We had time.

After ordering and handing Logan his caffeine, I scowled. "Now stop bitching and wake the fuck up."

He was eyeing me, more wary now. "You think Dad's mixed up with something?"

I shrugged, rolling to a stop at a stoplight. "Who the fuck knows. I just didn't like hearing that guy speak our dad's name and connecting dots to everyone else we love in that bar."

"Channing will handle him. That's his world."

I knew that. Or I was trying to tell myself I knew that.

But...

"It's a feeling. You heard what that kid said last night. Channing's sister stuck around because of a feeling."

"And you got one of those too?"

I dipped my head down. "I do. Yeah."

Logan swore, "Well, shit then."

"Yeah."

That was all we spoke until we pulled into the country club's parking lot. I turned for the golf course and pulled in beside our dad's Bentley. Logan got out with his coffee. Not me. For some reason, I wanted my hands free, didn't like the feeling I was getting for that either, but here we were anyways.

Logan sipped his coffee, eyeing me as he fell in step next to me. "Can't beat anyone up, you know."

I cursed, "You telling me or reminding me?"

"Both. I recognize that look you got going. Normally, I'd be all aboard for it, but not here. Not with Dad."

I shot him a hard look. "Like I don't fucking know that."

He grinned, taking another drink. "Love you, bro. Don't know if I say it enough."

I paused, looking right at him.

Shit. This kid.

He was a year younger than me. We'd gone through hell and back, and he was *still* at my side.

"I love you too, bruh."

"Bruh." He scowled. "What the fuck? I'm not a bruh. I'm a bro. Get your terms right, jeez, old man."

"What do you usually say? 'My bad?'"

Logan started laughing. "Jackass."

"That shit, I learn from you."

He laughed harder, tipping his head back.

Yeah. It felt nice doing this with Logan.

Spotting their cart, we had to walk two hills.

Logan said as we did, "Taylor wants to move back here after law school."

I slowed my pace. "That's what you want?"

He lifted up a shrug, finishing his coffee. "She wants to be around her dad. I want to be around you guys."

"Sam and I talked about getting a house here."

"Really?"

I nodded. "For the off-season, and that's if I don't get traded."

"You shouldn't."

"You never know with wide receivers. Salary caps and shit."

"That's messed up."

"That's business."

He grunted, "True." Then he changed the subject, "Something's up with Nate."

"I know."

"Is he talking to you?"

"We talk, but he's not said much. Just that stuff is shifting in his family."

Nate was a touchy subject for both of us. I wasn't sure where to step and where not to step, and I didn't know what Logan all knew either.

Finally, Logan just sighed. "He's never opened up much about his family, not his siblings. He just hated his parents. That's all I remember from back then."

"I know."

Logan's voice grew distant. "You ever feel we weren't there for him? Not as we should've been?"

I stopped, facing him. The dad stuff could wait. This conversation just took priority.

"What are you saying?"

Logan sighed, looking off over the golf course, but I doubted he was seeing any of it. "I've heard a little, and what I've heard makes me feel like we weren't there. Not like he was for us. We were caught up in our lives, dealing with our shit. We didn't help him with his shit."

"Nate didn't ask."

Logan shook his head. "Negative. That doesn't stand. We should've been there—"

"He came back when we had Sam with us. We were taking care of her, then her psychotic mother was trying to put me in jail. Nate came back, but he had an attitude. He never talked. He never asked. He was there and he was pissed, and some of that was because we had Sam. Are you forgetting that shit?"

"No, but—"

"But nothing. Nate and I were close. He was there for me, and I've never forgotten that, but brother, he came back and he wasn't quite the same. Our lives were falling apart. Broudou. The girls putting Sam in the hospital. Nate was in the hospital—"

"He went in because of us."

"Yeah, because he was around. Because we were friends, but I asked. I was there, but I was only there as much as he would let me. He didn't let me. He was fucking a girl who wanted to hurt Sam. He chose the fraternity over me. Don't think I didn't note that shit, because I did. I saw it. I watched it, and I asked. No one knew I did, but I did. I couldn't help because Nate didn't want help. And he was doing shit that put him against us. I had to choose what line to stand on, and there's never a question. I stand with Sam and I stand with you. Always. Even if I have another brother bleeding, but if he's on the other side and if I cross that line and it hurts you, or Sam? Then I can't cross the line."

I knew what Logan was talking about, some of it happened not long ago, and this needed to be hashed out right here and now.

"I love Nate. Our friendship goes in waves, but I'll always have love for him. But I repeat, this is no excuse, but you cannot help if they are not open, and I'm not talking where you kick down a door. I'm talking a cement wall, backed up with landmines and a tunnel to get away. Nate is closed off. Deep down, he's closed off, and until something makes that open up, no one can get in. Not really."

Logan shifted back on his heels. "He's not closed off with me."

"Yeah, he is. You just never realized it."

It was a shot at my brother, but fuck. I took it.

His eyes flared.

He received it.

"You fuck."

"Maybe. Ask him about his brother, then you'll get it."

He tipped his chin up, his nostrils flaring. "Maybe I fucking will."

"Then you fucking do that."

"Mason? Logan?"

We'd gotten distracted, so distracted that our dad got the jump on us.

Crap.

Logan snorted in laughter, and I knew I'd never live that down. And turning, there he was, walking toward us. A golf cart was behind him on the trail, their caddy at the wheel and the guy he was golfing with in the back. All watching us.

"You guys are in town?" James smiled at us, and the kick was that he seemed genuine.

A part of me was loath to even go down this line of questioning, but I had to. Things had gotten better between him and both Logan and me, Analise and Sam as well, but there was still a whole frosty layer of anger I had toward him. Maybe not anger. Maybe just distrust?

My dad was someone you couldn't trust, even his own kid.

I knew that was a golden rule long ago, so I stamped all the annoying shit down inside of me and faced off against James Kade.

I just needed a look. That's all I was searching for.

So, I threw out the first bait. "Ran into a Maxwell last night."

I stopped, watched.

Nothing.

James seemed confused. There was no reaction. At my silence, he prodded, "Maxwell?"

Logan had eased back. He was letting me take the lead.

"He runs a motorcycle club."

There. His mouth flattened. He eased back a step, but caught himself.

He knew him, or he knew about the club.

"Really? That's interesting."

"Fuck, Dad. At least sound convincing." From Logan.

James tossed him an annoyed look before focusing back on

me. "What's this about? We should have lunch. Is Samantha here? Maddie? Analise would love to see her granddaughter."

"Fucking hell, Dad!" Logan exploded. "She's not my goddaughter's grandmother. Malinda is. That's it. Helen ain't. Analise ain't. You're all proxied uncles and aunts and shit, but not her grandparents. That's reserved for Sam's dad and Malinda."

James' eyes flared.

He was going to say something.

I got in there first. "We were going to get our asses kicked last night, Dad."

Another flare, but he liked hearing me say that. I could still be a manipulative bastard. Good to know. I'd have to take an extra shower later.

I kept going, "He heard who we were, asked if we were your sons, and then he called his boys off. Now I want to know why he did that." I tipped my head to the side. "You in business with a motorcycle club?"

He didn't answer.

"They're outlaws, Dad."

Logan was toying with him too, though it was more of a taunt coming from him.

James lowered his head, cleared his throat, and readjusted the brim of his golf hat. "Look, I'm not appreciating what you're inferring, but you're wrong. It's the opposite, actually. If you think he let you go because of me, that wasn't the case. A ways back, when we first moved in, we pulled business from some of the smaller towns. Yes, that happened. I was blamed, but it wasn't my fault. That's like asking a businessman not to do business. I do business. That's what I'm good at, but yeah, there were some locals who were angry with us."

What the fuck was he talking about?

"Dad." Logan's voice was like steel.

Both of us turned to him.

He was locked on James, his look harsh. "I'm good at what I'm learning to do. Reading between the lines, and what you're not saying isn't making me proud to be your son."

James flinched at that. He coughed again, raising his head up. "The two of you haven't been proud to be mine for a long time. Hearing that now only saddens me because I thought there'd been progress—"

"Are they suing you?"

I hadn't thought of that, but Logan was locked in on our dad. He smelled a trail and was following it down the path.

James was silent. That gave us the answer.

"Shit, Dad. That's why they backed off." Logan shook his head. "I'm sure some of it was because of Channing, but I bet if they harmed the sons of the guy they're going after in court, that'd hurt their lawsuits."

Again, silence from James.

"Christ, Dad."

"What do you want me to say? People get sued. There'll be a settlement. There's always a settlement."

Now I was reading between the lines. "They won't settle, will they?"

And remembering back last night, how the older guy presented himself, how he spoke, how Channing had been alarmed on the phone last night, none of that was sitting well with me.

Our dad seemed to already be pleading the fifth.

"Shit. They won't."

"They're a motorcycle club. They can't touch us."

"Let's hope they can't, Dad, because what if they could?" Logan whistled under his breath. "Intelligent outlaws. Nothing scarier, right?"

James looked at a loss for words, but then he sighed. His voice lowered. "I won't let anything hurt you guys, or Sam, or Taylor, or Maddie. Nothing. This is a matter that's being settled in court.

They have no case. They've just been like mosquitos. They won't go away, that's all."

I'd heard enough.

My stomach was tightening. "Whatever, Dad."

His eyes skirted between us. "So, uh. Can we do lunch? Analise really would like to see little Maddie."

I was already turning and walking away.

I heard Logan say behind me, "No, Dad. No lunch, but it was good to see you."

Me, I didn't say a word. There wasn't any more *to* say.

We got to the rental and I cursed once the doors were closed. "Bet you a fucking mil that he ran those towns, whatever towns he's talking about, dry. He ruined businesses. Families lost their jobs. I don't want to think about the collateral to kids. Shit. Shit, Logan!"

And I was putting two and two together, and I wasn't liking what else was connecting.

"What are you thinking?"

"I'm thinking I need to have a phone call with Channing about this MC."

"No, Mason." Logan's tone was assertive, final. I rarely heard this from him. "Not this road. Not this fight. It isn't ours. It's his and I don't want to go where that road might take us. Not this time."

He wasn't asking, or pleading. He was saying.

He added, "You had a feeling. Well, so do I. About this. We have to leave this one alone. We're good. What we have coming ahead of us is nothing but good. Let's stay *that* course, not go down this course."

Since he brought it up, in a roundabout way, I had to take this opening.

I asked, "You okay? And I mean you and Taylor?"

He got quiet. "Why are you asking?"

"Sam's worried. You're quieter than normal."

"Oh." He seemed to consider the question. "Yeah. I mean, you grow up and change. Like I said before, I think Taylor and I need to think about some things, but we're good. She and I. There just comes a time when you have to strike out and start your own course, your own family. I think I'm getting there, but yeah. To answer your question, we're good." He gave me a half-grin. "Love you, brother."

"Love you too."

Talk time was done. I turned the engine on, and we went back.

And as for staying our courses, I listened to my little brother.

18

SAMANTHA

Mason crawled back into bed and woke me up.

His mouth went right between my legs, and I came awake like I'd never come awake before. It was another form of heaven, and then he proceeded to take me there.

I'd just come down when he eased out and settled beside me, but still caressing me. He was peppering kisses on my throat, up my jawline, then back down to my mouth. I curved into him, deliciously satiated and knowing no part of my body wanted to move. Except my boobs.

Because I had to pump. Again.

And then I remembered and shoved his face away. "Maddie."

"Is with Malinda. She's taking care of her."

I wanted my baby, but my other baby was here and we were heading back to Massachusetts today. That meant the real world.

I sighed, nuzzling into Mason as he held me. "I want my little girl."

He grinned, his mouth finding mine before he pushed himself up. "Then I'll get your little girl."

"Do it with clothes, please."

He'd been reaching for the handle, then paused. Throwing

me a rakish grin, he grabbed some pants and hauled them on. "Forgot we weren't home. And alone."

A moment later, he was returning with Maddie in his arms. Pure bliss. Right there.

I sat up and he handed her off, and the world was perfect all over again. She was awake and alert, her little hands reaching up as Mason shifted back into bed beside me. He leaned over, cooing and playing with his little girl as I held her.

It was a bit later when Mason asked, "Did you get enough time with Heather?"

I nodded. I'd adjusted so I was lying further down in bed. Maddie was between us, her arms and legs kicking up in the air. She was trying to suck one of her toes.

"Yeah. I did. She's happy."

"She is."

I looked up. Mason was watching me, his eyes soft.

I murmured, feeling my throat swelling up, but knowing it was only good I was feeling, "Everyone seems happy."

Mason nodded, his eyes going back to Maddie. He laid his hand on her stomach, his palm down and he began tickling her. Her smiles and shrieks filled the air.

Those eyes of his, always soft when he looked at his little girl.

"I think everyone has their own path, and I think everyone will get to where we are."

"You think?" Because, God, I hoped so.

"I do."

He leaned over. I met him halfway and our lips brushed each other in the most tender kiss I've felt in a long time from him. It took the air out of my lungs for a second. I reached up, my hand cradling the back of his neck, and I tugged him closer. "I figure we have thirty minutes before Malinda breaks down our door for lunch."

He grinned against my mouth. "I figure you're right."

We were right.

Lunch was wonderful, but then again, the whole weekend had been wonderful.

I couldn't wait for our next visit back.

If you enjoyed Fallen Crest Campout, please leave a review! They truly help so much.

FOR MORE READING

If you'd like more Mason and Sam, go to
www.tijansbooks.com
for a bonus scene previously written and released.

Make sure to grab Crew for free for a limited time!

Books still to come:
Always Crew
(the conclusion of the Crew series)

Nate's book
(late winter 2020/early spring 2021)

AUTHOR NOTE

I hope you enjoyed catching up with the Fallen Crest and Crew characters!
Thank you to all the readers who love these characters and keep them alive, especially in my reader group.

CREW

CHAPTER ONE

You aren't supposed to want to die.

I know that's isn't what society wanted to hear. It isn't supposed to be felt or thought about. It's supposed to be ignored, but I was standing here. I was watching my crew beat the crap out of a guy, and all I wanted was to trade places with the guy.

I knew that sounded morbid. I did, and I'm not talking about the off-the-cuff comment like you bombed your history exam and it's the "kill me now," or your boyfriend dumped you and "Gur-rrrl, I just wanna dieeee! WTF?!"

No. I was talking about the *dark* kind where it's in the back of your mind, where it's a small little door that you wanted to open and disappear through . . .

Some days, it was hard to suppress and harder to ignore, so I wasn't doing either of those.

"You're not going to touch my sister again," Jordan growled before delivering probably his fourth punch already. "Got it, *asshole*?"

It was my face getting bloodied. Not that guy. That's what was going on in my head, but not anyone else. Not Jordan, who straightened to sneer at the guy laying at his feet.

Jordan Pitts.

He was the self-proclaimed leader of our crew. Note here: *self-*proclaimed. As in, he announced it one day. No one took objection and off he went, embracing his cocky swagger thinking he speaks for our group of four. The truth was that he did, but only when we didn't have a problem with what he was saying.

Our group wasn't a dicktatorship, whether he believed that or not.

Jordan bent down, his long, six-feet-two self, grabbed a hold of the guy's shirt and lifted him in the air. He shook him, growling again in his face, but the guy couldn't answer. His face was broken. Literally. Either Cross or Jordan had punched his cheek so hard it looked busted. His whole face was a mess of blood and bruises. I would've felt sorry except for two things: he tried to rape Jordan's sister, and when Jordan asked him to report himself, he added a curse word, his middle finger, and he spat on Jordan's shoes.

Apparently this guy didn't know the reputation of either us, or Jordan himself. If he had, he would've ran the other way when he met Mallory Pitts. You had to give the guy some props. Instead of lying, he was honest. He told Jordan exactly what he thought of that suggestion. And anyway, if he'd lied, we would've followed up, and if he didn't report himself, this whole beat-down would've happened anyway.

This was my crew.

After Jordan, but there were two others besides myself. Cross Shaw, Zellman Greenly.

My name is Bren Monroe and even though I'm in the middle of this whole dark diatribe, and even though we're looking like the bad guys right now, things aren't always as they seem.

Jordan slammed the guy back down to the ground, then bent over him to issue more threats.

Cross stepped back, and I felt his gaze on me even before I looked up. Yes, there it was. His tawny hazel eyes that so many girls loved. We were family—and not that kind of family. But I'd have to be blind, and even then I probably would've still understood why so many girls at Roussou High salivated over him.

Six one. Lean, but built. He had a strong square jawline, one that he would clench at times. A face that was almost prettier than mine. He was one of those types of guys. He would be gorgeous even if he was a girl, a fact I loved to tease him about. But teasing aside, the facts were simply put: Cross got the girls. He could just show up somewhere, and ten would be at his side. He could nod at a girl, and she'd go to his side for the night, usually be down for anything he wanted. Cross was the quiet, nice guy....except he wasn't really either of those at all. I mean, he was, but he wasn't. He was generally quiet, but he talked to me. And he was nice, but he could be lethal. Piss him off, and you'd never see him coming. He wasn't like Jordan with the growling and throwing people around. He'd come right up to you, and then you'd be waking up in the hospital a couple days later.

And while I loved Jordan and Zellman, they weren't Cross.

They weren't my best friend, the guy whose closet I'd crawl into so many nights when I needed a sanctuary from my own hell called home.

I met his eyes as he came toward me. His golden hair and tanned skin made him every pretty boy's nightmare. When would he wake up and realize he had more potential than all of us? He could go to New York and be a model, or go to Hollywood and be a teen actor. Why he stayed in Roussou was beyond me.

He wasn't messed up like the rest of us. He wasn't messed up like me.

"You got the look," he said, coming to stand next to me.

Yeah. I knew what he was referencing, but I didn't respond.

"Okay, fuckhead," Jordan announced. "We're going to leave you now, and if you think you'd like to turn any of us in, don't forget what we have on you. Got it? Nod your head, dickwad."

Jordan was the intellectual here. He was smrt.

The guy made a gurgling sound and managed to move his head a bit.

It sufficed for Jordan, and he nodded. "Good." He turned, his long legs crossing the ground toward us.

I leaned against the back bed of his truck, Cross still next to me, as Jordan opened the driver's side door.

Zellman had been standing nearby at the ready. That's what he tended to do any day of the week—always behind Jordan and waiting. Since Jordan had come over to us now, so did Zellman. He launched himself up to the opened truck bed behind us.

I heard the cooler open, and he tossed a beer Jordan's way. "Bren? Cross?" he called.

Cross shook his head.

I turned around to look at the guys. "I'm good. Thanks."

"You sure?" Zellman extended a beer.

"I am."

Jordan's eyes flicked upwards—his response to a lot of the things I did. We had each other's backs, but to Jordan that meant doing everything he wanted. Sometimes we disagreed, and every time I didn't do what he did, he took it that I was disagreeing with him.

Family doesn't work that way.

I watched him, just for a moment.

One day we would battle.

One day it would be me against him.

One day his disapproval would make me snap, or one day he wouldn't *just* be a jerk because I wasn't doing what he wanted. He would go too far and that would be the day I'd meet him halfway.

I already knew how the lines would shift in our group. Cross would back me up. Zellman would probably back-up Jordan. It'd be two against two so when that day would happen, I hoped to be in a really piss-ass poor mood because even though I was the only girl in the group, one of the two only girls in the entire system, I could handle my own and I wanted to enjoy lighting into Jordan on that day. But that day wasn't today, and I hoped it would take a long time to come. I did care for Jordan like a brother, though he wasn't my actual blood.

"So." Jordan slammed the door shut again, the force rocking his truck for a second. He propped up a leg on the truck's gutter. "What's the plan for tonight?"

It was the last night before our senior year started.

Sunday night. People had been to church this morning, and we'd beaten someone bloody this evening. There was irony in there somewhere. I was just too tired to find it.

"Ryerson has a party tonight," Zellman offered. "I say we go." His shaggy curls bounced around as his blue eyes darted between all of us.

"Yeah?" Jordan's eyes lit up.

Zellman nodded. "I'm down to go. I think Sunday Barnes got new boobs this summer." He grinned. "I'm hoping to check 'em out personally."

Jordan laughed. "I'm good with that." He tipped his head back, finishing his beer, and then tossed the bottle into the trees behind us. "Bren, Cross, what about you guys?"

Cross would wait for me, so I said, "I'm good for the night."

"No party?"

"I'm gonna head home."

Jordan's disapproval settled in the air over us, but no one said a word.

"Think I'm down with you guys for the party," Cross added after a moment.

Zellman thrust a fist in the air. "Hell yeah. Take it." He offered his half-emptied beer.

Cross laughed, but shook his head. "I'll wait for the good liquor there. Ryerson always has something."

"Yeah! That's what it's about." Zellman finished his beer, and reached into the cooler for a second one. "Jordan?"

"I gotta drive." He glanced to me. "Ride home?"

I looked over to where the guy still lay on the ground. He hadn't moved.

I shook my head. "Think I'll walk. I can cut through the trees."

"You sure?"

Cross moved around us, clapping Jordan on the shoulder. "Let's go. Bren can take care of herself." He glanced back to me, circling around the front of the truck to get into the passenger side. He knew I wanted to be on my own tonight. He knew it because he could feel it. Just like I could almost hear his thoughts now.

She always has.

I finished in my own head, *Always will.*

Cross' statement seemed to settle the other guys, and Jordan started the truck. He circled around me, kicking up a cloud of dust, and zoomed back down the way we'd come. He saluted me with a finger as he passed by. Zellman had settled in the bed, sitting by the cooler, and he held up his beer as his goodbye.

I shook my head, the smallest hint of a smile tugging at my mouth, but that was all the reaction they got out of me.

Once they were gone, it was just me, the bloodied guy, and the same dark quiet I'd felt earlier.

It came out of nowhere at times, swallowing me whole. Some days it would vanish just as quick, others like tonight, it lingered.

It used to scare me. I now missed it at times when it wasn't there, but I always knew it would move on. It was like a firefly slipping away into the night. When that happened, I was left with the feeling that I let something slip from my fingers.

This night, that firefly remained. It warmed me.

Make sure to grab Crew!

CPSIA information can be obtained
at www.ICGtesting.com
Printed in the USA
BVHW041730300420
578958BV00012B/97